**KT-389-746**

## St. Helens Libraries

Please return / renew this item by the last date shown.
Books may also be renewed by phone and Internet.

Telephone – (01744) 676954 or 677822
Email – centrallibrary@sthelens.gov.uk
Online – http://eps.sthelens.gov.uk/rooms

| | | |
|---|---|---|
| 30 JUL 2021 | | |
| IZR SEP 2021 | | |
| A16 - - FEB 2022 | | |
| D1 | | |

# WED FOR THE
# SPANIARD'S
# REDEMPTION

# WED FOR THE SPANIARD'S REDEMPTION

CHANTELLE SHAW

MILLS & BOON

First published in Great Britain 2019
by Mills & Boon, an imprint of HarperCollins*Publishers*
1 London Bridge Street, London, SE1 9GF

Large Print edition 2019

© 2019 Chantelle Shaw

ISBN: 978-0-263-08295-1

**MIX**
Paper from
responsible sources
**FSC** **FSC™ C007454**
www.fsc.org

This book is produced from independently certified FSC™ paper to ensure responsible forest management. For more information visit www.harpercollins.co.uk/green.

Printed and bound in Great Britain
by CPI Group (UK) Ltd, Croydon, CR0 4YY

For Adrian.
Being a writer's husband is no easy job!
Love you.

# CHAPTER ONE

## *Spanish Stud's Sex Romp with Cabinet Minister's Wife!*

RAFAEL MENDOZA-CASILLAS SCOWLED as he sifted through the pile of newspapers on his desk. All the tabloids bore similar headlines, and even the broadsheets had deemed that it was in the public interest to report his affair with Michelle Urquhart.

The story wasn't only in the UK. All across Europe people were eating their breakfast while studying a front-page photograph of the heir to Spain's biggest retail company entering a top London hotel late at night accompanied by the voluptuous Mrs Urquhart. A second photo showed him and Michelle leaving the hotel by a back door the next morning.

*One can only speculate on how Europe's
most prolific playboy and the Minister's
wife spent the intervening hours!*

That was one journalist, writing in a particularly tacky tabloid.

'It is one scandal too many, Rafael.'

Hector Casillas's strident voice shook with anger and Rafael held his phone away from his ear.

'On the very day that the company's top-selling Rozita fashion line launches a new bridal collection *your* affair with a married woman is headline news. You have made the Casillas Group a laughing stock.'

'I was not aware that Michelle is married,' Rafael said laconically when his grandfather paused to draw a breath.

Not that her marital status interested him particularly. He was not responsible for other people's morals—especially as his own morality was questionable. But if he'd known that Michelle's husband was a public figure he would not have slept with her. Even though she had made it clear that she was available within minutes of him meeting her in a nightclub.

Rafael never had a problem finding women to occupy his bed and, frankly, Michelle had not been worth this fallout.

He leaned back in his chair and watched the rain lash the windows of his office at the Casillas Group's UK headquarters in London's Canary Wharf. The Casillas Group was one of the world's largest clothing retailers, and as well as Rozita the company owned several other top fashion brands.

Rafael visualised his grandfather sitting behind his desk in the study of the opulent Casillas family mansion in Valencia. There had been many occasions in the past when he had been summoned to that study so that Hector could lecture him on his failings and remind him—as if Rafael needed to be reminded—that he was part *gitano*. The English word for *gitano* was gypsy, and in other areas of Europe the term was *Roma*. But the meaning was the same—Rafael was an outsider.

'Yet again you have brought shame on the family and, even worse, on the company,' Hector said coldly. 'Your mother warned me that you had inherited many of your father's faults. When I rescued you from the slums and brought you into the family I intended that you would succeed me as head of the Casillas Group. You are my grandson, after all. But sadly there is too much of your father's blood in you, and tacking Casillas on to your name does not change who you are.'

Rafael's jaw clenched and he told himself he should have expected this dig. His grandfather never missed an opportunity to remind him that he did not have the blue blood of Spanish nobility running through his veins. His father had been a low-life drug dealer, and his mother's relationship with him, a rebellion against the Casillas family's centuries-old aristocratic heritage, had ended when she'd fled from Ivan Mendoza, leaving behind Rafael and his baby sister in a notorious slum on the outskirts of Madrid.

'The situation cannot continue. I have decided that you must marry—and quickly.'

For a moment Rafael assumed that he had misheard Hector. 'Abuelo…' he said in a placating tone.

'The board want me to name Francisco as my successor.'

A lead weight dropped into the pit of Rafael's stomach. 'You would put a *boy* in charge? The Casillas Group is a global company with a multi-billion-dollar annual turnover. Frankie would be out of his depth.'

'Your half-brother is twenty and in a year he will finish studying at university. More importantly he keeps his pants on.'

Bile burned a bitter path down Rafael's throat. 'Has my mother put you up to this? She has never made it a secret that she thinks her second son is a true Casillas and should be the heir to the company.'

'No one has put me up to anything. I make my own decisions,' Hector snapped. 'But I share the concerns of the board members and the shareholders that your notoriety and frequent appearances in the gutter press do not reflect well on the company. Our CEO should be a man of high principles and an advocate of family values. I am prepared to give you one more chance, Rafael. Bring your wife to my eightieth birthday celebrations at the beginning of May and I will retire from my position as Chairman and CEO and appoint you as my successor.'

'I have no desire to marry,' Rafael gritted, barely able to control his anger.

'In that case I will appoint your half-brother as my heir on my eightieth birthday.'

'*Dios!* Your birthday is six weeks from now. It will be impossible for me to find a bride and marry her in such a short time.'

'Nothing is impossible,' Hector said smoothly. 'Over the last eighteen months you have been introduced to several high-born Spanish women and any one of them would be a suitable wife for you. If you want to be my heir badly enough you will present your bride to me and we will have a double celebration to mark my landmark birthday and your marriage.'

Hector ended the call and Rafael swore as he threw his phone down on the desk. The old man was crazy. It was tempting to think his grandfather had lost his marbles, but Rafael knew that Hector Casillas was a shrewd businessman. The CEO-ship had been passed down to the next generation's firstborn male since Rafael's great-great-great-grandfather had established the company, one hundred and fifty years ago.

Hector Casillas's only offspring had been a daughter so Rafael, the oldest grandson, was next in line. But he knew that many on the board of directors and many of his relatives were not in favour of an outsider—which was how they regarded him—being handed the reins of power.

Hector's words taunted him. *'If you want to be my heir badly enough...'* Rafael bared his teeth in a mirthless smile. Becoming CEO of the company was the *only* thing he wanted. Being named as his grandfather's successor had been his dream, his obsession, since he was a skinny twelve-year-old kid who had been taken from poverty into the unimaginably wealthy lifestyle of his aristocratic family.

He was determined to prove that he was worthy of the role to his detractors, of whom there were many—including his mother and her second husband. Alberto Casillas was his mother Delfina's second cousin, which meant that their son Francisco was a Casillas to his core. Like that of many aristocratic families, the Casillas gene pool was very exclusive, and the majority of Rafael's relatives wanted it to stay that way.

But the retail industry was going through big changes, with increasing focus on internet sales, and Rafael understood better than most of the board members that the Casillas Group must use innovation and new technology so that it could continue to be a market leader. His grandfather had been a great CEO but now new blood was needed.

*But not a gitano's blood*, taunted a voice inside him. Once he had begged for food like a stray dog on the filthy streets of a slum. And, like a dog, he had learned to run fast to avoid his father's fists.

Rafael shut off the dark memories of his childhood and turned his thoughts to the potential brides his grandfather had mentioned. He'd guessed there must be an ulterior motive when his mother had invited the daughters of various elite Spanish families to dinner parties and insisted that Rafael should attend. But he hadn't taken the bait which had been dangled in front of him and he had no intention of doing so—despite Hector's ultimatum.

He would have to marry, but he would choose his own bride. And it would *not* be a love match, he thought cynically.

A psychologist would probably suggest that Rafael's trust issues and avoidance of commitment stemmed from his being abandoned by his mother when he was seven. The truth was that he could forgive her for deserting *him*, but not for leaving his sister, who had been a baby of not even two years old. Sofia's distress had been harder for him to bear than his father's indifference, or the sting of Ivan Mendoza's belt across the back of Rafael's legs.

His determination to gain acceptance by the Casillas family was as much for his sister as for himsef. He *would* be CEO and he was prepared to offer a financial incentive to any woman who would agree to be his temporary wife.

Once he had achieved his goal there would be no reason to continue with his unwanted marriage, Rafael brooded as he grabbed his briefcase and car keys and strode out of his office.

His PA looked up when he stopped by her desk. 'I'm going to my ten o'clock meeting and I should be back around lunchtime,' he told her. 'If my grandfather calls again tell him that I am unavailable for the rest of the day.' He paused on his way out of the door. 'Oh, and, Philippa—get rid of those damned newspapers from my office.'

The day couldn't get any worse, surely?

Juliet chucked her phone onto the passenger seat of the van and slid the key into the ignition. She wouldn't cry, she told herself. After she had lost her parents in the car accident which had also ended her dancing career she'd decided that nothing could ever be so terrible that it would warrant her tears.

But today had started disastrously, when she'd read a letter from an Australian law firm informing her that Bryan intended to seek custody of Poppy. A knot of fear tightened in her stomach. She couldn't lose her daughter. Poppy was her reason for living, and even though her life as a single mum was a struggle she would fight with the last breath in her body to keep her little girl rather than hand her over to her father, who had never shown any interest in her until now.

A phone conversation with her business partner Mel a few minutes ago had been the final straw on this day from hell. *Her life was falling apart!*

Juliet watched the rain streaming down the windscreen and blinked back her tears. There was no point sitting here in the car park behind the Casillas Group's plush offices in Canary Wharf. She still had sandwich deliveries to make to other offices in the area. Her business, Lunch To Go, might be facing ruin, but her customers had paid for their sandwiches and wraps and they were expecting her to turn up.

She sniffed as she started the engine and pulled her seat belt across her lap before putting the van into gear and pressing her foot down on the accelerator pedal. But instead of moving forward the van lurched backwards, and there was a loud bang followed by the tinkling sound of broken glass.

For a split second Juliet couldn't think what had happened. But when she looked in her rear-view mirror it was obvious that she had reversed into the car which had swung into the parking bay behind her.

And not just any car, she realised with mounting horror. The sleek gunmetal-grey Lamborghini was one of the most expensive cars in production—so Danny, the parking attendant who allowed her to park her van in this car park, which was reserved exclusively for Casillas Group executives, had told her.

The day had just got a whole lot worse.

She watched the owner of the Lamborghini climb out of his car and stoop down to inspect the front bumper. Rafael Mendoza-Casillas: managing director of the Casillas Group UK, international playboy and sex god—if the stories about his love-life which regularly appeared in a certain type of newspaper were to be believed.

Juliet's heart collided with her ribs when he straightened up and strode towards her van. The thunderous expression on his handsome face galvanised her into action and she released her seat belt and opened the driver's door. God, she hoped the damage to his car wasn't too bad or too expensive to repair. A claim on her vehicle insurance would bump up her premium next year.

'*Idiota!* Why did you try to reverse out of your parking space? If you'd had the sense to use your mirror you would have seen that I had parked behind you.'

His gravelly voice with its distinct Mediterranean accent was clipped with anger. But it was the sexiest voice Juliet had ever heard and her skin prickled with awareness of the man who towered over her.

She was five feet four—the minimum height for dancers in the *corps de ballet*—and she had to tilt her head so that she could look at him. His eyes were an unusual olive-green, glinting furiously in his tanned face. And what a face. Juliet had caught sight of him occasionally at the Casillas Group offices, when she'd been delivering sandwiches, but he hadn't so much as glanced at her whenever she'd walked past him in a corridor. One time she'd entered the lift as he had stepped out of it and the sleeve of his jacket had brushed against her arm. The spicy scent of his aftershave had stayed with her for the rest of the day, and now her stomach muscles contracted when she inhaled his exotic fragrance.

'I'm not an idiot,' she muttered, stung by his superior tone and dismayed by her unbidden reaction to his potent masculinity.

The torrential rain was flattening his thick black hair to his skull, but nothing could detract from his film star looks. With chiselled features, razor-edged cheekbones and a square jaw shaded with dark stubble, he was utterly gorgeous. Beneath her apron, which was part of her uniform, Juliet felt her nipples tighten.

Heavy black brows winged upwards, as if he was surprised that she had answered him back. 'The evidence suggests otherwise,' he drawled. 'I hope your vehicle insurance will cover you for an accident on private land. This car park has a notice which clearly states that it is for the Casillas Group's senior staff's use only. You are trespassing, and if your insurance is not valid you can look forward to receiving a hefty repair bill for the damage you have caused to my car.'

Of course she would be covered by her insurance—wouldn't she? Doubt crept into Juliet's mind and her shoulders sagged. 'I'm sorry. It was an accident, as you said. I didn't mean to reverse into your car.' Panic swept through her. 'I don't have the money to pay for your repairs.'

The rain had soaked through her shirt and was dripping off her peaked cap. She remembered how excited she and Mel had been when they had ordered the red caps and aprons with their company logo on. They'd had such high hopes for their sandwich business when they'd started up a year ago, but the two bombshells Juliet had received today made it likely that now Lunch To Go would fold.

To make matters even worse, the most handsome man she'd ever set eyes on was now glaring at her as if she was something unpleasant that he'd scraped off the bottom of his shoe.

Misery welled up inside her and the tears that she'd managed to hold back until now ran down her cheeks, mingling with the rain. 'The truth is that I don't even have enough money to buy my daughter a new pair of shoes,' she said in a choked voice.

She'd felt so guilty when Poppy had said yesterday that her shoes made her toes hurt. And now there was a pain in Juliet's chest as if the oxygen was being squeezed out of her lungs. She couldn't breathe. She felt as if a dam inside her had burst, releasing the emotions she had held back for so long.

'I certainly can't afford to pay for work on your fancy car. What will happen if my insurance company refuses to pay for the damage?

I can't take out a bank loan because I already have debts...'

Her logical thought processes had given way to near hysteria. Ever since her parents had been killed in that horrific accident she had subconsciously been waiting for another disaster.

'Could I be sent to prison? Who would look after my daughter? If I'm deemed to be a bad mother Bryan will be allowed to take Poppy to Australia and I'll hardly ever see her.'

It was Juliet's worst fear and she covered her face with her hands and wept.

'Calm yourself,' Rafael Mendoza-Casillas commanded. 'Of course you won't go to prison,' he said impatiently as her shoulders shook with the force of her sobs. 'I am sure your insurance will cover the cost of the repairs to my car, and if it doesn't I will not demand money from you.'

Juliet's relief at his assurance was temporary. Her other problems still seemed insurmountable and she couldn't stop crying.

Rafael swore. 'We need to get out of this rain before we drown,' he muttered as he took hold of her arm and led her towards his car. He opened the passenger door. 'Get in and take a few minutes to bring yourself under control.' Moments later he slid into the driver's seat and raked a hand through his wet hair. He opened the glove box and thrust some tissues into her lap. 'Here. Dry your tears.'

'Thank you.' She mopped her eyes and took a deep breath. In the confines of the car she was conscious of his closeness. She smelled rain, and the cologne he wore. Another indefinable scent which was uniquely male teased her senses.

'I'm making your car wet,' she mumbled when she was able to speak. She was conscious that her rain-soaked clothes were dripping onto the car's cream leather upholstery. 'I really am sorry about damaging your car, Mr Mendoza-Casillas.'

'You can call me Rafael. My surname is a mouthful, don't you think?' There was an oddly bitter note in his voice. 'What is your name?'

'Juliet Lacey.' She supposed he needed to know her name and other details for the insurance claim.

Her eyes were drawn to his hard-boned pro-

file and a sizzle of heat ran through her, coun-
teracting the cold that was seeping into her
skin from her wet clothes. He glanced at her
and she quickly looked away from him. She
could not bear to think what she must look
like, wet and bedraggled, with her face blotchy
and her eyes red-rimmed from crying.

'I apologise for losing my temper. I did not
mean to frighten or upset you,' he said curtly.
'You said that you have a child?'

'Yes, a three-year-old daughter.'

'*Dios*, you can only be—what?—nineteen?—
and you have a three-year-old?' He sounded
faintly appalled. 'I assume that as you are not
wearing a wedding ring you're not married.'

'I'm twenty-four,' she corrected him stiffly,
'and, no, I'm not married. Poppy's father didn't
want anything to do with either of us when she
was born.'

'Who is this Bryan you mentioned?'

'He's Poppy's father. He has now decided
that he wants custody of her. Under Australian law both parents are responsible for their
child, even if they have never married or been
a couple. Bryan can afford the best lawyers

and if he wins the court case he intends to take Poppy to live in Australia with him.'

More tears filled Juliet's eyes and she scrubbed them away with a tissue.

'It's so unfair,' she blurted out. 'Bryan saw Poppy once when she was a baby. He told me he might have been more interested if she'd been a boy. But it's my word against his that he rejected his daughter. His lawyers are twisting everything to make it seem as though I refused to allow him to see his child. But I only brought Poppy back to England because Bryan insisted he wanted nothing to do with her.'

Juliet had no idea why she was confiding in Rafael when she didn't know him, and she was sure he wouldn't be interested in her problems. But there was something strangely reassuring about his size and obvious strength, the air of power that surrounded him. Words had tumbled from her lips before she could stop them.

'I've heard through my cousin, who lives in Sydney, that Bryan is dating the daughter of a billionaire and he wants to marry her. Apparently his girlfriend can't have children of her own because of a medical condition, but she desperately wants a child. My guess is that Bryan hopes to persuade his heiress to marry him if he can present her with a cute little daughter.'

Juliet bit her lip. 'Eighteen months ago Poppy spent a few weeks in temporary foster care when I had to go into hospital. She was very happy staying with the lovely family who looked after her. But somehow Bryan has found out that Poppy was fostered and he's using it as proof that I can't give her a secure upbringing and she'll be better off living with him.'

'Couldn't someone in your family have looked after your daughter while you were in hospital?'

The anger had gone from Rafael's voice and the sexy huskiness of his accent sent a little tremor through Juliet.

'My parents are dead and my only other relatives live in Australia. My aunt and uncle were kind to me when I stayed with them after my parents died, but they have busy lives and I try to manage on my own.'

'Why are you short of money?' Rafael turned his head towards her and Juliet felt his gaze sweep over her cap and apron. 'I take it that you have a job? What do the initials LTG stand for?'

'Lunch To Go is my sandwich business, which I co-own with my business partner. We've only been running for a year and our profit margins have been low while we have been getting established.' She gave another sniff and crumpled the soggy tissue in her hand. 'Things are finally looking up. But today I was called in by your HR manager and told that the contract we have to supply sandwiches to the Casillas Group's staff will finish at the end of the week because a new staff canteen is to open.'

Rafael nodded. 'When I established the London headquarters of the company it was always my plan to open a restaurant and a gym in the basement of the building for staff to use in their lunch break. The construction work took longer than anticipated and I asked HR to make a temporary alternative arrangement for staff to be able to buy their lunch from an outside source but still be subsidised by the company.'

'I didn't know about the staff restaurant,' Juliet said dully.

She'd never been down to the basement level—although she had overheard a couple of secretaries talking about the new staff gym. Her contract with the Casillas Group only required her to be given a week's notice.

'Will losing the contract have an impact on your business?'

'It will halve our profits,' she admitted heavily. 'I thought we could advertise for new customers at other offices—although a number of other food delivery companies have started up in this area, and the competition is high. And then I spoke to my business partner after my meeting and Mel told me she's going to sell the bakery shop where we're based. Her decision is for personal reasons—she and her husband want to move out of London. Mel owns the shop, and I can't afford to buy it or rent a new premises.'

'If your business closes what will you do?'

She shrugged. 'I'll have to look for another job, but I don't have any qualifications, or training in a career, and it will be almost impossible to earn enough to cover childcare for Poppy.'

Juliet thought of the home study business degree she had started but had had to abandon because she hadn't been able to afford the fees for the second year. That degree would have enabled her to find a better-paid job, or at least given her knowledge of the business strategies which would have been useful to develop Lunch To Go. But without Mel she simply could not manage, either financially or practically, to run the sandwich business.

Rafael was drumming his fingers on the steering wheel and seemed to be deep in thought. He had beautiful hands. Juliet imagined his tanned hands sliding over her naked body, those long fingers curving around her breasts and caressing the sensitive peaks of her nipples. Heat swept through her and she was startled by her wayward thoughts.

Bryan had broken her heart when he'd dumped her the morning after she'd given her virginity to him. A month later, when she'd tearfully told him that she was pregnant with his baby, his cruel rejection of her and her unborn child had forced her to grow up fast. She had felt a fool for falling for his easy charm and had vowed never to be so trusting again.

Being a single mother had left her little time to meet men, and it was a shock to discover that she could still feel sexual awareness and desire. Perhaps she was attracted to Rafael because he was so far out of her league that there was no chance that anything would come of it—a bit like a teenager with a crush on a pop star they were never likely to meet in real life, Juliet thought ruefully.

'I may be able to help you,' Rafael said, jolting her out of her reverie.

Her heart leapt. If he agreed to allow her to continue selling sandwiches to his office staff her business might just survive.

'Help me how?'

'I have an idea that would resolve your financial worries and also be advantageous to me.'

Juliet stiffened. 'What do you mean by "advantageous"?'

Was he suggesting what she thought he was? She knew that some of the women on the housing estate where she lived worked as prostitutes. Most of them were single mothers like her, struggling to feed their children on minimum wages. She didn't judge them, but it wasn't something she could ever imagine doing herself.

She put her hand on the door handle, ready to jump out of the car. 'I won't have sex with you for money,' she said bluntly.

For a few seconds he looked stunned—and then he laughed. The rich sound filled the car and made Juliet think of golden sunshine. She felt as if it had been raining in her heart since her parents had died and she'd been left alone. How wonderful it would be to have someone to laugh with, be happy with.

With a jolt she realised that Rafael was speaking.

'I don't want to have sex with you.'

His slight emphasis on the word *you* made Juliet squirm with embarrassment, which intensified when he skimmed his gaze over her. His dismissive expression said quite clearly that he found her unattractive.

'I have never had to pay for sex with any woman,' he drawled. 'What I am suggesting is a business proposition—albeit an unusual one.'

'I make sandwiches for a living,' she said

flatly, wishing the ground would open up and swallow her. 'I can't think what kind of business we could do together.'

'I want you to be my wife. If you agree to marry me I will pay you five million pounds.'

# CHAPTER TWO

'VERY FUNNY,' JULIET muttered, disappointment thickening her voice. 'I'm not in the mood for jokes, Mr Mendoza-Casillas.'

'Rafael,' he corrected her. 'And it's not a joke. I need a wife. A temporary wife—in name only,' he added, evidently reading the crucial question that had leapt into her mind. He stared at her broodingly. 'You have admitted that being a single parent is a financial burden. What if, instead of struggling, you could live a comfortable life with your daughter without having to work?'

'Some hope,' she said ruefully. 'I'd have to win the lottery to be able to do that.'

'Consider me your winning ticket, *chiquita*.'

His sudden smile softened his chiselled features and stole Juliet's breath. When he smiled he went from handsome to impossibly gorgeous. He reminded her of the male models on those TV adverts for expensive aftershaves—

only Rafael was much more rugged and masculine.

She tore her eyes from him, conscious that her heart was beating at twice its normal rate. 'You're crazy,' she told him flatly.

And so was she, to be still sitting in his car. Five million pounds! He couldn't be serious. Or if he was serious there must be a catch. She felt hot, remembering his amused reaction to her suggestion that he was offering to pay her for sex. God, what had made her say that? Many of today's newspapers had a photo on the front page of Rafael and a beautiful blonde woman with an eye-catching cleavage. Juliet glanced down at her shapeless figure. She looked like a stick insect compared to Rafael's latest love interest.

'If you need a wife why don't you marry your girlfriend, whose picture is all over the front pages of the papers?'

'For one thing, Michelle is already married—but even if she were free to marry me she would not be suitable. All of my lovers, past and current, would expect me to fall in love with them,' he said drily.

He was so arrogant! She wanted to come

back with a clever comment but she was mesmerised by the perfect symmetry of his angular features, which were softened a little by his
blatantly sensual mouth.

'But you're not worried that *I* might fall in
love with you?' She'd intended to sound sarcastic, but instead her voice was annoyingly
breathless.

'I don't recommend that you do,' he said in
a hard voice. 'I do not believe in love,—or
marriage, for that matter. I'm not crazy,' he
insisted. 'I have a genuine reason for needing
to be married.'

He swore when his phone rang, and then
took his mobile out of his jacket pocket and
cut the call.

'We can't talk now. I'll meet you this evening
and we can discuss my proposition.'

She shook her head. 'I'm not interested.'

'Not interested in earning yourself five million pounds for being my wife for a couple of
months?' He reached across her and put his
hand over hers to prevent her from opening the
car door. 'At least give me a chance to explain,
and then you can make up your mind whether
I'm crazy or not. Although, frankly, you would

be foolish to miss out on the chance to earn a life-changing amount of money. Think what you could do with five million pounds. You would never have to worry about the cost of buying your little girl a pair of shoes ever again.'

'All right.' Juliet released a shaky breath. He was relentlessly persuasive. She couldn't think properly when his face was so close to hers that as he leaned across her body she was able to count his thick black eyelashes. 'I'll meet you to discuss your proposition, but I'm not saying that I'll agree to it.'

She pressed herself into the leather seat, hoping he would not notice the pulse at the base of her throat that she could feel thudding erratically. It would add to her humiliation if he guessed that she was attracted to him—especially as he quite obviously did not feel the same way about her.

'It will have to be after nine,' she told him. 'I work the evening shift as a cleaner at a shopping centre close to where I live.'

Juliet felt a mixture of relief and disappointment when Rafael straightened up and moved away from her.

He handed her a business card. 'Here is my phone number. Text me your address and I'll collect you from your home at nine-fifteen.' He frowned. 'What about your daughter? Does someone look after her while you are at work in the evenings?'

'Of course I have childcare for Poppy. I certainly wouldn't leave her on her own,' she said indignantly, stung by his implication that she might be an irresponsible mother.

It was the accusation that Bryan's lawyer had levelled against her, and remembering the custody battle she was facing over her daughter evoked a heavy sense of dread in the pit of her stomach.

Five million pounds would enable her to hire her own top lawyer to fight Bryan's claim on Poppy, Juliet thought as she climbed out of Rafael's car and ran through the rain back to her van. But she would be nuts even to consider the idea.

Rafael parked his Lamborghini outside a grim-looking tower block and his conviction that it had been a mistake to suggest to a woman he had never met before today that she should marry him grew stronger. He visualised Juliet Lacey, who had resembled a drowned rat when he'd shoved her into his car out of the rain. Her voluminous apron had covered her figure, but from what he'd been able to see she was skinny rather than curvaceous. Her face had been mostly hidden behind by the peak of a baseball cap that was surely the most unfeminine and unflattering headwear.

In Rafael's opinion women should be elegant, decorative and sexy, but the waif-like sandwich-seller failed on all counts. His fury that she had damaged his beloved Lamborghini had turned to impatience when she'd burst into tears. He was well aware of how easily women could turn on the waterworks when it suited them. But as he'd watched Juliet literally fall apart in front of him he'd felt a flicker of sympathy.

He had heard a woman sob brokenly only once before, in the slum where he had spent the first twelve years of his life. Maria Gonzales had been a neighbour, a kind woman who had often given food to him and his sister. But Maria's teenage son had been drawn into one of the many drug gangs who'd operated in the slum and Pedro had been stabbed in a fight. Rafael had never forgotten the sound of Maria's raw grief as she'd wept over the body of her boy.

When Juliet had told him of her financial problems and her fear that she might lose custody of her young daughter the idea had formed in his mind that she would make him an ideal wife. The money he was prepared to pay her would change her life, and more importantly she would have no expectations that their marriage would be anything other than a business deal.

Maybe he *was* crazy, Rafael thought as he climbed out of his car and glanced around the notoriously rough housing estate—a concrete jungle where the walls were covered in graffiti. A gang of surly-looking youths were staring at his car, and they watched him suspiciously when he walked past them on his way into the tower block. He guessed that the older male in the group, who was wearing a thick gold chain around his neck, was a drug dealer.

Rafael had grown up in a shanty town on the outskirts of Madrid, where dire poverty was a breeding ground for crime and lawless gangs ruled the street. His father had been involved in the criminal underworld, and as a boy Rafael had seen things that no child should see.

His jaw tightened as he took the lift up to the eleventh floor and strode along a poorly lit walkway strewn with litter. The tower block was not a slum but a sense of poverty and deprivation pervaded the air, as well as a pungent smell of urine. It was not a good place to bring up a child.

Juliet and her young daughter were not his responsibility, he reminded himself. But it was hard to see how she would turn down five million pounds and the chance to move away from this dump.

He knocked on the door of her flat and it opened almost immediately. Rafael guessed from the unbecoming nylon overall Juliet was wearing that she must have returned from her cleaning job only minutes before he'd arrived. Without the baseball cap hiding her face he saw that she had delicate features, and might even have been reasonably pretty if she hadn't been so pale and drawn. Her hair was a nondescript brownish colour, scraped back from her face and tied in a long braid. Only her light blue eyes, the colour of the sky on an English spring day, were at all remarkable. But the dark shadows beneath them emphasised her waif-like appearance.

A suspicion slid into Rafael's mind, and when Juliet took off her overall to reveal a baggy grey T-shirt that looked fit for the rag bag he studied her arms. There were none of the tell-tale track marks associated with drug addiction.

He flicked his gaze over cheap, badly fitting jeans tucked into scuffed black boots and thought of glamorous Camila Martinez, the daughter of the Duque de Feria and his grandfather's favoured contender to be Rafael's bride.

The difference between aristocratic Camila, who could trace her family's noble lineage back centuries, and Juliet, who looked as if she had stepped from the pages of *Oliver Twist*, was painfully obvious. It would show his grandfather that he was not a puppet willing to dance to the old man's tune if he turned up at Hector's birthday party and announced that he had married this drab sparrow instead of a golden peacock, Rafael mused, feeling a flicker of amusement as the scene played out in his imagination.

'I told you to call me when you arrived and I would meet you outside the flats,' Juliet greeted him. 'If you've left your car on the estate there's a good chance it will be vandalised. There's a big problem with gangs around here.'

Rafael shuddered inwardly at the thought of his Lamborghini being damaged. 'This area is not a safe place for you to be out alone at night,' he said gruffly, thinking that she must have to walk through the estate in the dark every evening when she'd finished her cleaning shift.

He looked along the narrow hallway as a door opened and a small child darted out.

'Mummy, where are you going?'

The little girl had the same slight build and pale complexion as her mother. She stared at Rafael warily and he was struck by how vulnerable she was—how vulnerable they *both* were.

Juliet lifted her daughter into her arms. 'Poppy, I've told you I'm going out for a little while with a…a friend and Agata is going to look after you.'

An elderly woman emerged from the small sitting room and gave Rafael a curious look. 'Come back to bed, *kotek*. I will read to you and it will help you to fall back to sleep.' She took the child from Juliet. 'The baby will be happy with me. Go and have the nice dinner with your friend.'

'Who is looking after your daughter?' Rafael asked when Juliet followed him out of the flat and shut the front door behind her. She had pulled on a black fake leather jacket that looked as cheaply made as the rest of her outfit.

For a moment he wondered what the hell he was doing. Could he *really* marry this insipid girl who looked much younger than mid-twenties?

But her air of innocence had to be an illusion, he reminded himself, thinking of her illegitimate child. And besides, he did not care what she looked like. All he was interested in was putting a wedding ring on her finger. Once he had fulfilled his grandfather's outrageous marriage ultimatum he would be CEO of the Casillas Group. He did not anticipate that he would spend much time with his wife and would seek to end the marriage as soon as possible.

'Agata is a neighbour,' Juliet said. 'She's Polish and very kind. I couldn't do my cleaning job if she hadn't agreed to babysit every evening. Poppy doesn't have any grandparents but she loves Agata.'

'What happened to your parents?'

'They were killed in a car accident six years ago.'

Her tone was matter-of-fact, but Rafael sensed that she kept a tight hold on her emotions and her breakdown earlier in the day had been unusual.

'I believe you said that you have no other family apart from some relatives in Australia?'

She nodded. 'Aunt Vivian is my mum's sister. I stayed with her and my uncle and three cousins, but they only have a small house and it was a squeeze—especially after I had Poppy.'

So Juliet did not have any family in England who might question her sudden marriage, Rafael mused as they stepped into the lift. Once again he imagined his ultra-conservative grandfather's reaction if he introduced an unmarried mother who sold sandwiches for a living as his bride. It would teach Hector not to try to interfere in his life, Rafael thought grimly.

The lift doors opened on the ground floor and he took hold of Juliet's arm as they passed the gang of youths, who were now loitering in the entrance hall and passing a joint between them.

'Why do you live in this hellhole?' he demanded as he hurried her outside to his car. 'It can't be a good place to bring up a child.'

'I don't live here out of choice,' she said wryly. 'When Poppy was a baby we lived in a lovely little house with a garden. Kate was my mum's best friend, and the reason why I left Australia and came back to England was because she invited me and Poppy to move in with her. She was a widow, and I think she enjoyed the company. But Kate died after a short illness and her son sold the house. I only had a few weeks to find somewhere else to live. I had already started my sandwich business and needed to live in London, but I couldn't afford to rent privately. I was lucky that the local authority offered me social housing. Living on this estate isn't ideal, but it's better than being homeless.'

She ran her hand over the bonnet of the Lamborghini. 'You are a multi-millionaire—you can have no idea about the real world outside of your ivory tower.'

*You think?*

Inexplicably Rafael was tempted to tell her that he understood exactly what it was like to live in poverty—wondering where the next meal was coming from and struggling to survive in an often hostile environment. But there was no reason why he should explain to Juliet about his background. He dismissed the odd sense of connection he felt with her because they both knew what hardship felt like. His childhood had given him a single-minded determination to get what he wanted, and Juliet was merely a pawn in the game of wills with his grandfather.

He opened the car door and waited for her to climb inside before he walked round to the driver's side and slid behind the wheel.

'I know that five million pounds could transform your situation and allow you to provide your little girl with a safe home and a very comfortable lifestyle free from financial worries.' He gunned the Lamborghini away from the grim estate and glanced across at her. 'I'm offering you an incredible opportunity and for your daughter's sake you should give it serious consideration.'

It occurred to Juliet as she sank into the soft leather seat of the sports car that this might all be a dream and in a minute she would wake up. Things like this did not happen in real life. A stunningly handsome man offering her five million pounds to be his wife was the stuff of fantasy and fairy tales.

She darted a glance at Rafael's chiselled profile and felt a restless longing stir deep inside her. It was a long time since she had been kissed by a man, and she'd never felt such an intense awareness of one before.

Bryan had been her first and only sexual experience. She'd spent her teenage years at a boarding ballet school, and although she'd known boys, and danced with them, she had been entirely focused on her goal of becoming a prima ballerina and hadn't had time for boyfriends.

The scholarship she had been awarded had paid the school's fees, but there had been numerous other costs and her parents had scrimped and saved so that she could follow her dream. She'd always felt that she owed it to her mum and dad to succeed in her chosen career.

But the car accident which had taken her parents' lives had left Juliet with serious injuries—including a shattered thigh bone. The months she'd spent in hospital had intensified her sense of isolation and loneliness.

She had been painfully naïve when she'd met Bryan Westfield, soon after she'd moved out to Australia to stay with her aunt Vivian and uncle Carlos. She'd been looking for someone to fill the hole in her heart left by her parents' deaths, and blonde good-looking Bryan had seemed like 'the one'—until she'd realised he had only wanted sex.

'You're not the first young woman to have your heart broken and be left with a baby and you won't be the last,' Aunt Vivian had said briskly when Juliet had admitted that she was pregnant.

Her aunt had meant well but Juliet had felt

stupid, as well as bitterly hurt by Bryan's rejection, and she'd vowed never to lay herself open to that level of pain again. It made her reaction to Rafael's undeniable sexual magnetism all the more confusing.

The look of distaste that had flickered over his face when she'd opened the door to him wearing her cleaning overalls had made her shrivel inside. She knew from photographs of him in gossip magazines—invariably with a blonde glamour model or actress hanging on to him—that she was as far from his ideal woman as the earth was from Mars. But his lack of interest in her made it easier to consider his proposition.

'You said I would be your wife in name only? Does that mean the marriage would not be...' she hesitated '...consummated?'

She was thankful that her scarlet cheeks were hidden in the dark interior of the car. If he laughed she would die of mortification.

'Physical intimacy between us will not be necessary,' he said coolly.

He did not actually state that he wouldn't touch her with a barge pole but the message was clear. Juliet swallowed, feeling ashamed that the gorgeous man beside her found her repellent. They were both wearing jeans, but his were undoubtedly a designer brand, and she'd noted when he had walked around to his side of the car how the denim clung to his lean hips. His tan leather jacket looked as if it had cost the earth, while her clothes came from a discount store and her boots had seen three winters.

With a sigh, she turned her head and stared out of the window.

'We're here.'

Rafael's voice pulled Juliet from her thoughts and she discovered that he had turned the car onto the driveway in front of a large and very beautiful house.

'Where is "here"?' she asked when he switched off the engine.

'My home in England—Ferndown House. It's too dark to see now, but the house backs on to Hampstead Heath.'

Juliet looked down at the rip in her jeans. 'I suppose you don't want to be seen with me in public when I look like this,' she said flatly.

He turned his head towards her but she could

not bring herself to look at him and see his disdainful expression.

After a moment he sighed. 'I brought you to my home because we will be assured of privacy while we talk, which we would not be in a bar or restaurant. There is no shame in being poor. It is obvious that you work hard to provide for your daughter, but I can help you. We can help each other. Now, come inside and meet my housekeeper. Alice has prepared dinner for us.'

If Juliet could have designed her dream home Ferndown House would have been perfect in every way. From the outside it was a gothic-style Victorian property, but inside it had been cleverly remodelled and refurbished into a sophisticated modern house which still managed to retain many original period features.

She caught her breath when Rafael showed her one huge room, with a stunning parquet floor and floor-to-ceiling mirrors on one wall.

'The previous owners enjoyed hosting parties in here, but I don't entertain very often and the room is not used much,' he told her.

The room would be an ideal dance studio, Juliet thought. It was her dream to one day own a ballet school, and she visualised ballet *barres* along the walls and a box of the powdered chalk called rosin on the floor, for dancers to rub onto their pointe shoes to help stop them slipping.

She followed Rafael along the hall and looked into another reception room, a study, and a library that overlooked the garden. Outside lighting revealed a large, pretty space with wide lawns, where Poppy would love to play. Juliet gave a faint sigh, thinking of the couple of rusty swings in the playground on the housing estate where she sometimes took her daughter.

Upstairs on the second floor they walked past what she guessed was the master bedroom, with a four-poster bed. Juliet carefully avoided Rafael's gaze as she wondered how many women had spent the night with him in that enormous bed.

'There is a nursery along here,' he said, leading the way along the corridor. He opened a door into a large room with painted murals of fairies on the walls and laughed at her startled expression. 'I'm not planning to fill the nursery with my own children, but my sister has four-year-old twin girls who sometimes come to stay here.'

They went back downstairs to the dining room, where a cheery fire burned in the hearth and velvet curtains were drawn across the windows.

'You have a beautiful home,' Juliet murmured when Rafael drew out a chair at the table and waited for her to sit down before he took his place opposite her.

He was silent while Alice served a first course of gooey baked brie with warm pears. Then the housekeeper left the main course on a heated trolley for them to serve themselves and Rafael poured wine.

'If you agree to my proposition Ferndown House will be yours and your daughter's home for the duration of our marriage. When, after a few months, the marriage is dissolved, five million pounds will be transferred into your bank account and you will be able to buy a property of your own. Have you any ideas about where you would like to live?'

'Somewhere on the coast,' she said instantly. 'When I was a child my parents took me on holiday to Cornwall a few times. We stayed in a caravan next to the beach.' Memories of a happy childhood full of love and laughter tugged on her heart. 'I've always thought how wonderful it would be for Poppy to grow up by the sea.'

'Agree to my deal and you can make your dreams reality,' Rafael said in a softly persuasive tone.

Excitement fizzed inside Juliet, overriding the voice of caution in her head. With the money that Rafael was offering she could buy a little cottage with a garden and a sea view. She didn't want a mansion—just a place that she and Poppy could call home. But what Rafael was asking was *wrong*, her conscience whispered. Marriage should be a life-long commitment. Her parents had enjoyed a happy marriage and, although Juliet had learned a harsh lesson with Bryan, she still hoped that one day she would fall in love with someone special who would love her in return.

She took a small sip of her wine, determined to keep her wits about her. 'I'm curious to know why you need a wife so badly that you're prepared to fork out five million pounds for one.'

'My grandfather has demanded that I marry before he steps down as head of the Casillas Group and appoints me as CEO of the company and Chairman of the board of directors,' Rafael said curtly. 'The dual roles have been passed down to the eldest son for generations. My mother does not have any siblings, which means that I am the next firstborn male and I should be Hector's successor. *Dios*, it is my *birthright.*'

He slapped his hand down on the table and Juliet flinched.

'Why does your grandfather want you to marry?'

'He disapproves of my lifestyle.'

She nodded. 'You do have a reputation as a playboy, and your affair with the wife of a prominent politician was reported in most of today's newspapers.'

'I spent one night with Michelle two months ago. The paparazzi must have seen us leave the nightclub together and go to a hotel, but those pictures did not appear in the papers the next day.' Rafael's jaw hardened. 'My guess is that someone paid the photographer to delay offering the pictures to the tabloids until the day the Casillas Group's biggest-selling retail line Rozita launched a new bridal collection.'

Juliet stared at him. 'Why would anyone do that?'

'It could have been a competitor, hoping to damage the company's reputation, or more likely someone who wanted to blacken my name and convince my grandfather that I would not be a responsible CEO.'

'Do you have any idea who?'

'In all probability it was someone on the Casillas Group's board who does not support my claim to be Hector's successor, or one of my relatives for the same reason.'

'How awful that someone in your own family might have betrayed you,' Juliet murmured. 'Families are supposed to support one another.'

Rafael stared at her broodingly. 'The pursuit of power is a ruthless game, with no place for weakness or emotions,' he said harshly.

While he served their main course of chicken cooked in a creamy sauce Juliet played his words over in her mind and felt a little shiver run through her. She had no doubt that Rafael was ruthless, and he must be utterly determined to become CEO if he was prepared to pay such an incredible amount of money for a wife.

*Could she do it?* His proposition had seemed crazy at first, but now she understood that his grandfather was forcing Rafael to marry. What he was suggesting was a business deal, she told herself.

The chicken was delicious, and a welcome change from the cheap, microwavable ready meals she tended to live on because fresh, good-quality produce was so expensive. She concentrated on eating her dinner, glad of the distraction.

Rafael got up to throw another log on the fire. The flames crackled and an evocative scent of applewood filled the room. The wine, the food and the general ambience of the room was helping Juliet to relax, and she gave a soft sigh.

'Can you honestly tell me that you're not tempted?'

Rafael's seductive voice curled around her. She took another sip of her wine.

'Of course I'm tempted. To be honest I can't even *imagine* having five million pounds. It's an unbelievable sum of money and it would certainly transform my life. But I have to consider what is best for Poppy. I'm worried that she might become attached to you while we're married and be upset when we divorce and you're no longer around.'

Rafael frowned. 'I think that scenario is extremely unlikely. Immediately after our marriage you and Poppy will accompany me to Spain to attend my grandfather's eightieth birthday party. I will present you as my new wife to Hector and he will announce me as his successor. The transition of power will take a little while—maybe a month or two—and we will need to attend a few social engagements together to show the Casillas board members and shareholders that I have reformed my playboy lifestyle since my marriage,' he said sardonically. 'After a suitable period of time you and your daughter will be able to return here to Ferndown House—we'll make the excuse that you prefer her to attend a nursery school in England. It will be necessary for me to spend much of my time at the Casillas Group's headquarters in Valencia, and the truth is that I won't come to England very often.'

'How romantic.'

Juliet told herself it was stupid to feel disappointed that Rafael had made it clear he would avoid her as much as possible.

'I am not offering you romance,' he said in a hard voice. 'I want you to be my wife for no other reason than to fulfil my grandfather's command that I must marry before he will make me CEO.'

He stood up and walked over to the sideboard, returning to lay some papers on the table.

'We are required to give twenty-eight days' notice of our intention to marry at the register office. My lawyers have prepared a contract stating that five million pounds will be transferred into your bank account when I succeed my grandfather as head of the Casillas Group. All you have to do is sign your name. I will take care of all the arrangements for our wedding, and for you and your daughter to move from your current home into Ferndown House.'

Juliet stared at the document in front of her and imagined Poppy running around the garden and playing with the dolls' house in the nursery.

She swallowed. 'It seems too easy.'

'It *is* easy. Everything will be as I have explained to you. There are no catches.'

Rafael's voice was like warm honey sliding over her. Tempting her. She wished her dad was around so that she could ask his advice—although she knew in her heart that he would advise her against marrying for money.

But five million pounds! Her heart was thudding so hard she was surprised it wasn't audible in the silent room. If she accepted Rafael's proposition her money worries would be over, but would she be selling her soul to the devil?

'I need time to think about it,' she whispered.

'I don't have the luxury of time. I have to be married by my grandfather's eightieth birthday, which is six weeks from now, or he will appoint my half-brother as his successor.' Rafael picked up a pen from the table and held it out to her. 'I am offering you a chance to give your daughter a better life. If you walk away now you will have thrown away that chance. I won't make the offer again and I will find another bride.'

The clock on the wall ticked loudly.

*Do it. Do it.*

Juliet snatched the pen from Rafael and signed her name where he showed her. It was for Poppy, she tried to reassure herself. A better future for her daughter.

'*Bueno!*' Rafael did not try to disguise the satisfaction in his voice. He picked up their wine glasses and handed Juliet hers. 'Let us drink a toast, *chiquita*, to the shortest marriage on record.'

# CHAPTER THREE

A MONTH HAD never passed so quickly—or so it seemed to Juliet.

For the first couple of weeks after she had agreed to Rafael's marriage proposition she had been busy winding down her sandwich business. Mel had found a buyer for the bakery shop and it had been an emotional moment as they'd closed the door for the last time.

'I'm intrigued to know more about your new business opportunity in Spain,' Mel had said. 'Why are you being so secretive?'

'I'll tell you more if it happens.'

Juliet hadn't revealed to her friend the true reason why she would be going to Spain. She was sure Mel would think she was mad if she explained that she had agreed to marry a man she did not know for money.

As the date of the wedding had drawn closer her doubts had multiplied. But Rafael had promised that there was no catch to their business deal.

Deciding what to tell Agata had been more difficult. Juliet was fond of the Polish woman who had helped her and Poppy so much, and after some soul-searching she'd told Agata the white lie that she was marrying Rafael after a whirlwind courtship.

Today, packing her's and Poppy's belongings hadn't taken long, and a member of Rafael's staff had come and taken the few cardboard boxes down to an SUV.

Juliet strapped Poppy into the child seat and as the car drove away from the estate on its way to Ferndown House she felt a mixture of relief, apprehension and excitement that refused to be quashed at the prospect of seeing Rafael again.

She had spoken to him once on the phone, when he'd called her to check some details he needed in order to complete the paperwork for their wedding. His gravelly voice with its sexy accent had made her feel hot all over, and she'd closed her eyes and pictured his devastatingly handsome face.

Remembering his disdainful expression

when he'd seen her wearing her cleaning overalls, she had taken a bit of time over her appearance today. The pink jumper that Agata had given her at Christmas lent some colour to her washed-out complexion, and the old tube of mascara she'd found at the back of the bathroom cabinet had still had enough in it to darken her pale eyelashes.

But when they arrived at Ferndown House Alice the housekeeper greeted Juliet and explained that Rafael had left the previous day for a business trip to America.

'He is not sure when he will be back but he asked me to give you his PA's phone number. Miss Foxton will answer any queries you might have.' Alice smiled at Poppy. 'I've made some cookies. Would you like one?'

Juliet tried to shrug off her disappointment at Rafael's absence. There was no reason for them to spend any time together. Their marriage would be a formality which would allow Rafael to become CEO of his family's company and he was paying her an astounding amount of money to be his temporary wife, she reminded herself.

And sitting alone in the elegant dining room

at Ferndown House, enjoying one of the delicious meals that the housekeeper had prepared, was a lot nicer than sitting in her flat with a microwaveable meal after Poppy had gone to bed—although she felt just as lonely.

Rafael finally phoned her the evening before they were due to marry the following day. 'My plane has just touched down in London and I'm going straight to the office,' he told her.

His gravelly voice had its usual effect of bringing Juliet's skin out in goosebumps.

'I don't know what time I'll get back to the house. Make sure you're ready to leave for the register office at ten-thirty tomorrow morning.'

On her way up to bed she wondered if he really was going to the office so late, or if he planned to spend the night with a mistress. Perhaps he wanted to enjoy his last night as a bachelor before he was forced into a marriage that he patently didn't want.

It was none of her business what he did, Juliet reminded herself.

There was no logical explanation for her dismal mood. In a few months' time she would have five million pounds in the bank—more than enough to buy a cottage by the sea and for her to establish her own dance school.

It was after midnight when she heard a car pull up outside the house, and when she hopped out of bed and ran across to the window her heart skipped a beat as she saw Rafael's tall frame unfold from his Lamborghini. The moonlight danced across his face, highlighting his chiselled jaw and sharp cheekbones.

Tomorrow he would be her husband.

Butterflies leapt in her stomach—nerves, she supposed. But around dawn she woke feeling horribly sick. Frequent trips to the bathroom followed, and the severe bouts of vomiting left her feeling drained.

She certainly did not look like a blushing bride, Juliet thought as she stared at her ashen face and lank hair in the mirror. It was ten o'clock and she needed to hurry up and get ready.

Choosing what to wear did not take her long. She lived in jeans or a denim skirt, and the only vaguely smart item of clothing she owned was a mustard-coloured dress she'd bought in a sale years ago when she had first moved to

Australia and needed something to wear to job interviews. The colour hadn't looked so bad in the Australian sunshine, but on a grey spring day in England it made her pale skin look sallow.

She would have liked to buy something pretty to wear on her wedding day, but since her sandwich business had closed down and she'd given up her cleaning job she hadn't had an income. Living at Ferndown House meant that she hadn't had to pay for food, but she'd spent the last of her money on new shoes for Poppy.

Juliet had no time to worry about her appearance when another bout of sickness sent her rushing into the bathroom, and she emerged feeling shivery and hot at the same time. Then she spent ten minutes searching for Poppy's favourite teddy, knowing that her daughter would not sleep at night without Mr Bear. Finally they were ready.

*Was she doing the right thing?*

It was too late for second thoughts now, she told herself. She had already given up her flat and her job. If she did not marry Rafael she would be homeless.

As Juliet walked down the stairs a wave of dizziness swept over her. She clung to the banister rail with one hand and held on to Poppy with the other.

Rafael strolled into the hall and an expression of horror flickered across his face as he studied her appearance, before he quickly schooled his features and gave her a cool smile. He looked utterly gorgeous in a grey three-piece suit that emphasised his broad shoulders and athletic build. His black hair was swept back from his brow and the designer stubble on his jaw gave him an edgy sex appeal that was irresistible.

'I couldn't afford to buy a new outfit for the wedding,' Juliet told him stiffly.

She wished the ground would open up beneath her feet when she caught sight of herself in the hall mirror. She hadn't had the energy to do anything fancy with her hair and it hung in a heavy braid down her back.

'You look fine,' Rafael assured her smoothly.

It was a blatant lie, she thought.

She wished she wasn't so agonisingly aware of him. Her breath snagged in her throat when he lifted his hand and lightly touched her face.

'Although I'm guessing from the dark circles beneath your eyes that you did not sleep well last night, he murmured. 'You will do very well,' he added, in a satisfied tone that puzzled her.

But then he hurried her out to the car and she was too busy strapping Poppy into the child seat to think about Rafael's odd statement.

From then on everything about the day had an air of unreality. The wedding ceremony took place in an unremarkable room at the council offices, and the two witnesses were Rafael's PA and his chauffeur.

Juliet had asked Agata to come to the register office to look after Poppy during the ceremony, and Poppy's joy when she saw Agata brought tears to Juliet's eyes. Her parents would have loved their little granddaughter as much as Poppy would have loved to have grandparents.

Rafael had told her that he had a large extended family and that several of his relatives, including his mother, lived at the Casillas family mansion in Valencia. Perhaps his mother would enjoy having a child around and would make a fuss of Poppy? Juliet hoped so.

She must have made all the right responses

to the registrar, and even managed to smile—although she felt numb and her voice sounded strangely disembodied. Rafael slid a gold band onto her finger and she tensed when he lowered his face towards hers. She realised with a jolt of shock that he was going to kiss her. She had secretly longed to feel his lips on hers, but not like this—not to seal their farce of a marriage.

His mouth was centimetres from hers, and she quickly turned her head so that he kissed her cheek. He frowned, and she guessed that no woman had ever rejected him before. But then the registrar was presenting them with the marriage certificate and Juliet felt as brittle as glass as she stepped into the corridor, hardly able to believe that she was now Mrs Mendoza-Casillas.

'I hope you know what you are doing,' Agata said when Juliet hugged her outside the register office. 'You told me that you fell in love with your husband at the first sight, but I do not see love between you.'

Somehow Juliet dredged up a smile. 'I'm very happy.' She tried to sound convincing. 'I'll bring Poppy to visit you soon.'

Rafael was uncommunicative in the limousine that took them to the airport, and once they had boarded his private jet he opened his laptop, saying that he needed to work.

Juliet devoted herself to keeping Poppy entertained during the flight, and by the time the plane had landed in Valencia and they were in a car on the way to his family home she had a thumping headache—although thankfully the sickness seemed to be over. Poppy was tired and fretful, and Juliet felt frazzled, and she was relieved when the car turned onto a long driveway.

'You didn't tell me you lived in a palace,' she said to Rafael in an awed voice as the Casillas mansion came into view.

Built over four storeys, the villa had white walls and tall windows gleaming in the bright afternoon sunshine. The car drove past manicured lawns and a huge ornamental pool and fountain before coming to a halt by the imposing front entrance which was framed by elegant colonnades.

Juliet knew, of course, that Rafael was wealthy, but travelling on his private jet and seeing his family's palatial home had made her realise that she'd entered a world of incredible luxury and opulence which was a million miles away from her tower block in one of London's most deprived boroughs, and from her life as a single mother.

They climbed out of the car and her tension escalated as she lifted Poppy out of the child seat and attempted to set her down on her feet. Tears ensued until she picked the little girl up again.

'Poppy is tired from travelling,' she told a grim-faced Rafael. 'I'd like to get her settled and give her something to eat.'

'You will be able to do that soon, but first I will introduce you to my family. My grandfather has arranged a reception to celebrate our marriage.'

Was it her imagination or did Rafael sound as tense as she felt?

She bit her lip as he strode up the steps leading to the front door of the villa, leaving her to trail behind him with Poppy balanced on her hip.

On the top step, he turned to her and frowned. 'Let me take the child. She is too heavy for you to carry.'

Juliet felt beads of sweat running down her face—which was strange, because she was shivering even though the sun was warm. Poppy clung to her like a limpet and shrank away from Rafael when he tried to take her into his arms.

A man whom she guessed was the butler opened the door and ushered them into the villa. Juliet's stunned gaze took in a vast entrance hall with pink marble walls and floor. Rafael placed his hand between her shoulder blades and propelled her forward as the butler flung open a set of double doors into another enormous room that seemed to be filled with people.

The hum of voices became quiet and silence pressed on Juliet's ears. An elderly man stepped out of the crowd and came to greet them—but the smile of welcome on his face faded and his eyes narrowed.

'Rafael, I understood that you would be bringing your new wife with you.' The man spoke in Spanish and his harsh tone sent a shiver through Juliet.

'Abuelo...' Rafael drawled. 'I would like you to meet my bride.'

There was a collective gasp from the people in the room and the old man swore. He flicked his sharp black eyes over Poppy before he spoke to Juliet in English. 'Were you a widow before you married my grandson?'

Confused by the question, she shook her head. 'No. I've never been married before.'

His implication suddenly became clear, and a terrible certainty slid into her mind when the man whom she realised was Hector Casillas glared at Rafael.

*'Tu esposa y su bastarda son de la cuneta!'* he hissed in a venomous voice.

He was white-lipped with anger, but his grandson laughed.

'What is the matter, Abuelo?' Rafael drawled. 'You demanded that I marry and I have done what you asked.'

'There is something you should know.'

Juliet's teeth were chattering so hard that she could barely get the words out. Anger burned like a white-hot flame inside her, but she was determined to control her temper in front of Poppy, who was running around in the little courtyard behind the kitchen. Her daughter had been subjected to enough ugly emotions from Rafael's grandfather.

Rafael. *Judas.*

'What should I know?' he said indifferently.

'I understand Spanish. I learned to speak the language when I lived with my aunt Vivian and her husband Carlos, who is Spanish by birth.'

His brows lifted. 'Ah...'

'Is that all you can say?' she choked.

She wanted to scream at him. Worse than her rage was her sense of hurt, which felt like an iron band wrapped around her chest that was squeezing the breath from her lungs.

'Your grandfather said that I am from the gutter and he called Poppy a bastard.' Juliet swallowed hard. 'Technically, I suppose it's true. Poppy's father did not offer to marry me when I fell pregnant, and he refused to have any involvement with his daughter when she was born. But I don't regret for one second having my little girl, and I will not allow your grandfather or anyone else to upset her.'

'My grandfather has very old-fashioned views.' Rafael gave a shrug. 'He is disappointed because he hoped I would marry the daughter of a duke. Hector sets great store on aristocratic titles,' he said drily.

'You threw me to the lions deliberately. Your grandfather said those awful things about me and you didn't defend me.'

It was not just raw emotion that was making it hard for Juliet to swallow. Her throat was sore and she recognised that the shivery feeling and her jelly-like legs were signs of a flu-like virus, the start of which must have been the sickness she'd experienced that morning.

'Mummy, can I give some yoghurt to the cat?'

She forced a smile for Poppy. 'I don't think cats eat yoghurt, darling. And I want you to sit down and finish your tea.'

Juliet lifted her daughter onto a chair at the wooden table in the shade of a pergola. Although Poppy could not have understood the things that had been said by Rafael's grandfather, she had sensed the tension in the room and burst into tears. Rafael had brought them to the kitchen and asked the cook to find some food for the little girl.

Luckily Poppy had been distracted when she'd seen a tabby cat in a pretty courtyard where terracotta pots were filled with a profusion of herbs.

While Poppy tucked into a bowl of fresh fruit and yoghurt, Juliet said in a low tone to Rafael, 'I don't understand why you chose me to be your wife if you knew that your grandfather would not approve of me.'

She stared at him and saw a ruthlessness in his hard-boned face that sent a shiver through her.

'That was the point, wasn't it?' she whispered. 'You were angry that your grandfather had insisted on you being married before he would make you CEO, so to pay him back you married a woman you knew he would despise—a single mother from the gutter.'

She was mortified to think of the vision she must have presented to Rafael's family, looking like Little Orphan Annie in her horrible dress and scuffed boots, with a child on her hip.

'You are not from the gutter.' Rafael sounded impatient rather than penitent.

'I come from a run-down council estate where the police have given up trying to arrest the drug dealers because there are too many of them,' she said flatly.

Juliet wasn't ashamed of her background. Her parents had worked hard in low-paid jobs to give her the chance to pursue her dream of being a ballerina. And most of the families living in that tower block were good people who struggled to make ends meet.

None of them had judged her for being a single mother—like Rafael's grandfather had and perhaps Rafael himself did. One thing was certain—she did not belong in the Casillas mansion with Rafael's sophisticated relatives.

'I can't stay here knowing that your family despise me,' she told him. 'More importantly, I don't want Poppy to meet your grandfather again. I'll book us onto the next available flight to England.'

She kept a credit card for extreme emergencies and her current situation definitely qualified as an emergency. Poppy had been terrified when Rafael's grandfather had shouted at them. But Juliet had no idea how she would pay the credit card bill, or where she would go when she reached London. Perhaps Agata would allow her and Poppy to stay at her flat for a few days.

'My grandfather will calm down,' Rafael told her. 'Even if he doesn't, you are my wife and there is nothing Hector can do about it.'

'You can't use me and especially not my three-year-old child as pawns in your row with your grandfather. I don't understand why such bitterness exists between the two of you. There is poison here in paradise and I want no part in an ugly war of wills between two men who have more money than people like me—people from the *gutter*,' she flung at him, 'can only dream of.'

She could tell from the way his dark brows slashed together like a scar across his brow that he hadn't expected her to stand up to him.

It was about time she grew a backbone, Juliet told herself grimly. But even though she had discovered the unedifying reason why Rafael had married her she still could not control the heat that coiled low in her pelvis when he pushed himself away from the wall that he had been lounging against and crossed the small courtyard to stand in front of her.

Too close, she thought, lifting her hand up

to her throat to try and hide the betraying leap of her pulse.

'You became part of this when you signed our marriage agreement and it is too bad if you don't like it,' he said curtly. 'Let us not forget that your motives were hardly altruistic, *chiquita*. You sold yourself to me for five million pounds.'

'I see now that I sold my soul to the devil.' She put her hand on his arm and felt the iron strength of sinew and muscle beneath his olive-gold skin. 'It's not too late to end this madness. We can have our marriage annulled.'

'And give up what should be mine?' Rafael gave a harsh laugh. 'I am afraid not. I will be CEO, whatever it takes. We are in this together.'

A violent shiver shook Juliet and she gripped the edge of the table as the ground beneath her feet lurched.

'What's the matter?' Rafael demanded. 'You're even paler than you were at the register office.'

'I've been feeling unwell all day,' she admitted.

She turned away from him and started to

walk across the courtyard, but the ground tilted and she felt herself falling. From a long way off she heard Rafael call her name.

She mustn't faint because Poppy would be frightened, she thought before blackness blotted out everything.

When he was growing up Rafael had learned to run fast—to escape his father's temper, or shopkeepers who chased him for stealing food, or to avoid the dealers who forced the slum kids to deliver drugs.

As an adult he still ran to escape his demons. His favourite route took him through the Albufera Natural Park, where a huge freshwater lagoon was separated from the sea by a narrow strip of coastline. There he could run along the beach before heading into the sand dunes and the pine forest beyond.

The Casillas mansion overlooked the beach, and right now Rafael, gazing out of an upper-floor window, would have liked nothing better than to be pounding along the shoreline, with the sea breeze ruffling his hair and the sun on his back. Running gave him the head space to find solutions to his problems—but there was no easy solution to the situation he found himself in, with a marriage that he had been forced into against his will.

There had even been a chance of a reprieve. It might not have been necessary to go ahead with the wedding at all. He would have paid Juliet off and thought it a small price to pay for his freedom.

An opportunity had arisen to buy out a popular American fashion brand, and Rafael had spent the past month in California, determined to secure the deal which would give the Casillas Group a major stake in the US clothing retail market. The acquisition would, he hoped, prove to the board members and shareholders that he *should* be CEO.

But even his success had not been enough to persuade his grandfather to withdraw his marriage ultimatum.

'A wife will be good for you. Now that you are thirty-five it is time for you to settle down and think about the future,' Hector had said when Rafael had phoned to tell him that the Casillas Group now owned the US fashion brand Up Town Girl. 'I am an old man, and when I die I want to be certain that the next generation of my family will lead the company into the future.'

If Hector believed that having great-grand-children would be ensured by forcing his eldest grandson to marry he was going to be disap-pointed, Rafael brooded. He had no burning desire to have children. His parents had hardly been ideal role models, and although he was fond of his nieces he was too driven by his ambition to believe that he could be a devoted parent like his sister, or like Juliet.

*His wife.*

*Dios.* He pictured the sickly waif who had occupied his bed for the past two nights while he slept on the sofa in his dressing room. He hadn't thought about what he would do with Juliet once he'd married her, and he resented his nagging conscience which insisted that he was now responsible for her and her child.

Damn his grandfather for issuing his ri-diculous marriage ultimatum. Rafael's jaw clenched. Once his temper would have made him lash out and punch something—or some-one. At fifteen he had been expelled from an exclusive private school for fighting with another pupil who had taunted him for his rough manners.

'You grew up in the gutter, Mendoza. You call yourself Casillas but everyone knows your father was a *gitano*.'

Rafael had wiped the grin off the other boy's face with his fists, but when he'd cooled off he'd felt ashamed of his behaviour. As a child he had often been on the receiving end of his father's violent outbursts, but he wanted to be a better man than Ivan Mendoza and prove to his grandfather that he deserved the name Casillas.

From then on he'd learned to control his emotions. *Don't get mad, get even* had become his mantra.

At a new school Rafael had ignored the boys who'd reminded him about his background. Instead of losing his temper he had focused his energy on his studies, determined to catch up on the education he'd missed while he'd lived in the slum.

That single-mindedness had seen him gain a master's degree from Harvard Business School before he had joined the Casillas Group in a junior role and worked his way up the company ladder.

He pulled his mind back to the present when a small hand slipped into his, and glanced down at Juliet's daughter. Poppy was an enchanting child, with a knack of disarming Rafael's defences which he would have sworn were impenetrable.

'Will you read me a story, Raf?'

He hunkered down in front of her. 'Go and find a book from the shelf. I'll read you a story and then we will go and see if your *mamà* is feeling better.'

Across the room Rafael caught his sister's amused expression.

'*Raf?*' Sofia murmured.

'My name is unfamiliar for the child, and hard to say, so she shortens it to Raf. I seem to have made a hit with her,' he said ruefully.

'"The child" has a name,' his sister reproved him. 'Poppy is younger than the twins and you are the only person she knows in a house full of strangers. It's hardly surprising that she wants to be with you while her mother—*your wife*—is too unwell to look after her.' Sofia sighed. 'What made you do it, Rafael?'

He did not pretend to misunderstand, or to try to convince his sister that his marriage was anything other than a calculated ploy which would give him what he wanted.

'Abuelo blackmailed me into choosing a wife by threatening to name Francisco as his successor if I did not marry. The CEO-ship should be *mine*—and not only by birthright. I don't feel a sense of entitlement,' he insisted. 'When I joined the company I started at the bottom—sweeping the floor in a warehouse. Hector did not want me to receive special favours just because I am his eldest grandson. I quickly rose through the managerial ranks because I worked harder than anyone else. I have *proved* my worth.'

Rafael's gaze met his sister's eyes, which were the same shade of olive-green as his own. Their unusual eye colour was a physical sign of the difference that set them apart from the rest of the Casillas family.

'You and I are still seen as outsiders. Especially me,' he muttered. 'You smile and say the right things, and you are not viewed as a threat to Madre's ambition to see her beloved

Francisco—the true Casillas heir, in her opinion—made CEO.'

Sofia moved to break up a squabble between
her two daughters. 'Ana, give the doll to Inez
if she was playing with it first. Your uncle says
he will read a story. Why don't you help Poppy
choose a book?'

She turned her attention back to Rafael.

'I'm sorry I wasn't here two days ago, when
you introduced your wife to the rest of the
family. Madre says the girl you have married is
so thin and pale perhaps she is a drug addict.'

*'Dios!'* Rafael growled, biting back a curse
when he caught his sister's warning look to
remind him that children were present. 'Juliet
fell ill with a gastric virus shortly after we arrived.'

He was angered by his mother's unjust accusation. But his conscience pricked. When he
had first met Juliet her hollow cheeks and extreme pallor had made *him* suspicious that she
was a drug user. And her drab appearance was
one reason he had picked her for his bride, he
acknowledged, feeling a faint flicker of shame
as he pictured her in the ghastly creased dress

she'd been wearing when he had introduced her to his grandfather.

He hadn't realised that she was ill when they had arrived at the Casillas mansion. With another stab of discomfort Rafael admitted to himself that he'd been busy taking a vicious pleasure in Hector's fury when he'd announced that the waif clutching her illegitimate child in her arms was his wife.

Juliet was as far removed from any of the high-society daughters of Spanish aristocratic families whom Hector had expected him to marry as chalk was from cheese. But her lack of sophistication did not warrant his family's scorn.

'Juliet is a devoted mother—which is more than can be said for *our* mother,' he said harshly. 'Delfina is embarrassed by us because we remind her that she was once married to a low-life drug dealer. Sometimes I think she would have preferred it if Hector *hadn't* found us and brought us into the family.'

Sofia looked at him closely. 'I hope you have not led your wife to believe that you are in love with her?'

'Juliet understands that we have a business

deal and she will be well recompensed after she has served her purpose.'

'Oh, Rafael,' his sister murmured. 'I worry about where your ruthless ambition will lead you. When can I meet your bride?'

He shrugged. 'Perhaps later today. The doctor I called in to examine her has said that the virus hit her hard. But the nurse reported that Juliet's temperature was nearly back to normal this morning and she should be well enough to attend Hector's eightieth birthday party on Saturday evening.'

When *he* would be named as his grandfather's successor, Rafael thought with satisfaction. He had met the old man's stipulation for him to marry and now it was time for Hector to publicly recognise his firstborn grandson as the true Casillas heir.

There was a knock on the door and the butler entered the nursery. 'Yes, Alfredo, what is it?'

'Señor Casillas wishes to speak to you,' the butler told Rafael. 'He is waiting for you in his study.'

# CHAPTER FOUR

RAFAEL LOOKED DOWN at Poppy, who was holding a book out to him, before he responded to the butler. 'Tell my grandfather that I am with my stepdaughter and I will be along in ten minutes.'

'Why do you have to antagonise Hector?' Sofia demanded when Alfredo had left.

'He needs to realise that I am not one of the yes-men he surrounds himself with,' Rafael muttered. 'I am sick of his attempts to manipulate me. Besides, I promised to read to Poppy.'

He had felt oddly protective of Juliet's daughter since the ugly scene with his grandfather when they had arrived at the house had upset the little girl.

'You and Abuelo are both too proud,' Sofia said impatiently. 'It's like a clash of bulls.'

She broke off as the nursery door was flung open.

Rafael glanced across the room and saw Juliet standing in the doorway. She was wearing a pair of baggy pyjamas that had faded to an indeterminate colour and her hair was scraped back from her white face.

'Where is my daughter?'

She gave a low cry when she saw Poppy, and flew across the room to scoop the little girl into her arms.

'Oh, munchkin, there you are. I was scared I'd lost you.' Juliet's relief was palpable and tears spilled down her cheeks as she looked at Rafael. 'I thought you had taken Poppy away. I woke up and I didn't know where she was. I thought…' She shook her head and hugged her daughter to her. 'I hope that no one has upset her. Your grandfather…?'

'Hector has not met Poppy again since we arrived two days ago,' Rafael assured her gruffly.

He was not completely heartless, and Juliet looked pathetic in her rag-bag clothes that hung off her angular body, with her face blotchy and wet with tears.

'As you can see, Poppy is quite safe. I have been taking care of her.'

*'You?'*

The mistrust in her voice exasperated him, but he felt uncomfortable as he remembered how she had accused him—rightly—of failing to defend her and Poppy in front of his grandfather.

'I am not an ogre,' he said curtly. But the wounded expression in Juliet's eyes made him feel like the evil villain in a Victorian melodrama.

'I can't believe that we have been here for two days,' she said unsteadily. 'What happened to me?'

'You have been ill with a virulent virus which gave you a high fever. The doctor I called in gave you medication to bring your temperature down and it knocked you out.'

Rafael did not add that the doctor had voiced his concern that Juliet was underweight and most likely undernourished, which had lowered her immune system, allowing the virus to take a hold.

'I don't remember putting my pyjamas on.' She looked at him with something akin to horror in her eyes. 'Did you undress me?'

'The nurse I hired put you to bed.'

*Dios*, Rafael thought irritably. Juliet had

sounded appalled at the idea of him taking her clothes off. It was not a response he'd ever had from a woman before.

He recalled that at their wedding, when the registrar had invited him to kiss his bride and for the sake of convention he had tried to brush his lips over Juliet's, she had turned her head away to prevent him from kissing her mouth. Her behaviour had been puzzling because he knew she was attracted to him. Rafael always knew.

Before he was twenty he had discovered that he could have any woman he wanted with minimum effort on his part. No doubt his wealth and the name Casillas were partly responsible for his popularity, but he indulged his high sex drive with countless affairs with women who understood that commitment was not a word in his vocabulary.

He wasn't interested in his poor, plain bride. Although those attributes were the reason he had married her, he acknowledged, feeling guilt snaking through him as he remembered the crushed look on her face when his grandfather had insulted her. How was he to have known that Juliet understood Spanish? Rafael asked himself irritably.

'Rafael, are you going to introduce me to your wife?' Sofia walked up to Juliet and held out her hand. 'I apologise for my brother's lapse in manners. You must be Juliet. I'm Sofia, and my daughters are Ana and Inez. The twins have had a wonderful time playing with Poppy. She really has been quite happy with Rafael and me and the nanny, Elvira.'

'I panicked when I woke up in a strange place and couldn't find her.' Juliet set Poppy on her feet and the fierce look of love on her face as she watched her daughter tugged on emotions buried deep inside Rafael.

He had long ago got over the fact that his mother did not love him and that his relatives—with the exception of his sister—resented his existence. He'd never felt that he belonged anywhere or with anyone, and he had assured himself that he did not care. No one had ever looked at him as though they would give their life for him…as if they loved him more than anything in the world.

'Rafael—quick!'

Sofia's urgent tone jolted him from his

thoughts and he sprang forward and caught Juliet as her legs crumpled beneath her. She weighed next to nothing, he thought as he carried her over to the door.

'You are not fully recovered,' he said, ignoring her attempts to slide out of his arms. 'You should be in bed. I'll ask the nurse to check your temperature and bring you something to eat.'

'Poppy will be fine with me,' Sofia assured Juliet. 'I'll read the girls a story.'

'As soon as I'm better—which I'm sure I will be by tomorrow—I want to take Poppy home,' Juliet told Rafael when he'd carried her into the bedroom and sat her on the edge of the bed.

She was a slip of a thing, perched on the huge bed like a little sparrow, he mused. But as he straightened up he noticed that her eyes were really a quite remarkable bright blue. His gaze dropped to her mouth, which was pulled down at the corners in a sulky expression.

'Where is home, exactly?' he asked sardonically. 'I made it clear when you signed the marriage contract that you cannot return to Ferndown House until after we have attended my grandfather's eightieth birthday party and he has appointed me as CEO.'

'I wish I'd never signed the contract. You said there were no catches, but you didn't tell me that you had chosen me as your bride to punish your grandfather,' she said in choked voice. 'You certainly didn't think about my feelings when your family looked at me as though I had crawled out of the gutter.'

Rafael ignored the prick of his conscience. 'I'm paying you five million pounds,' he reminded her harshly. 'It is regrettable that my grandfather spoke to you the way he did, but I'm sure you'll get over it when the money is in your bank account and you can buy yourself nice clothes and jewellery—whatever you want.'

'All I want is security for Poppy,' she whispered. 'I'm not interested in jewellery and clothes.'

'That much I can believe,' he muttered, flicking his gaze over her revolting pyjamas before he stalked out of the room, away from the accusing expression in Juliet's eyes that made him feel ashamed of himself.

*Dios*, she should be grateful that she and her

daughter would no longer have to live in poverty, Rafael brooded as he strode down the grand staircase.

His foul mood was not improved when he entered his grandfather's study and saw the company's senior lawyer, Lionel Silva, seated behind the desk next to Hector. Rafael strolled across the room and lowered himself into a chair facing the two men, resting his ankle across his opposite thigh. His appearance was relaxed but his instincts sensed trouble.

'Lionel, I am glad to see you,' he drawled. 'I presume my grandfather asked you here today to set in motion the transfer of the CEO-ship to me, now that I am married. It is what we agreed, did we not, Abuelo?'

His grandfather gave a snort. 'Once again you have disappointed me, Rafael. I cannot say that I am surprised, when you have so often proved to be a disappointment. But this time you have excelled yourself.'

Rafael felt a flare of irritation mixed with something raw that he assured himself wasn't hurt. He'd spent the past twenty-odd years trying to earn Hector's approval—hoping to win his grandfather's love—although he refused to admit as much even to himself. Now all he cared about was his right to be recognised as the Casillas heir.

'I trust you were not *disappointed* when I secured a deal to buy out the biggest clothing retail company on America's west coast?' he said drily. 'The acquisition puts Casillas Group among the top five largest apparel retailers in the world.'

'I do not dispute that your business acumen is impressive,' Hector barked. 'But, as I have said before, our CEO is the figurehead of the company—all the more so because the role is combined with that of Chairman. It is a position of great power and responsibility that requires a sense of humility—which you lack, Rafael.'

'I have met the condition you imposed on me and brought my wife to Spain in time for your eightieth birthday celebrations. How does that show a lack of humility?' Rafael said grittily.

'Do not insult my intelligence. You know that I expected you to make a good marriage, befitting the Casillas family's noble heritage, but you have deliberately sought to undermine me by marrying an unprepossessing girl. Your wife looks no more than a teenager and yet she already has one illegitimate child and no doubt lives off hand-outs from the state.'

'Juliet is in her mid-twenties and she has always worked to support her daughter.'

Fury simmered inside Rafael at his grandfather's unfair description of Juliet. But his conscience prodded him that his reason for marrying her *had* been to infuriate Hector by introducing an untitled and unsophisticated bride.

The lawyer cleared his throat as he picked up a printed document. 'This is the agreement between you, Rafael, and your grandfather, stating Hector's intention to name you as his successor following your marriage.'

Rafael nodded. 'I have given you a copy of my marriage certificate.'

'Yes, it seems to be legitimate,' Lionel murmured, studying the other document in front of him. 'Nevertheless your grandfather has expressed his concern that your marriage to Miss Juliet Lacey is in fact a marriage of convenience which you have entered into for the purpose of gaining benefit or advantage arising from that status. In other words, your marriage to Miss Lacey is a sham, meant to deceive Hector and persuade him to name you as his heir and the next CEO of Casillas Group.'

'The marriage is perfectly legal.'

Rafael's grip on his temper broke and he jerked to his feet, slamming his hands down on the desk. He noted that the lawyer flinched but Hector remained absolutely still. A clash of bulls, his sister had once said, describing his battle of wills with his grandfather.

'I have kept to my side of our agreement and I expect you to honour your word, Abuelo.'

'What do *you* know of honour?' Hector snapped. 'It is my belief that you do not intend your marriage to be a permanent arrangement and that once you are CEO you will seek a divorce. But the wedding took place in England, and under UK law you cannot apply for a divorce until you have been married for one year.'

Rafael stiffened. 'So? Where is this leading?'

His grandfather gave a smug smile.

'On my eightieth birthday this Saturday I will announce that you are my successor, as we agreed, but I will not step down until the date of the first anniversary of your marriage—and only then if I am convinced that your marriage is genuine rather than an attempt to trick me.'

Hector gave Rafael a sly look.

'I am certain that there will be no need for me to try to prove or disprove the validity of your marriage A year will, I suspect, seem like a lifetime to a playboy such as you are, to maintain the pretence of a committed relationship with your unappealing bride.'

'You can't do that,' Rafael gritted. 'You agreed—'

'I can do whatever I think best protects the interests of the Casillas Group,' Hector interrupted. 'If I handed the company over to you and you divorced after only a few months of marriage it would suggest that you lack commitment. Instead I will appoint you CEO-in-waiting, and it will make sense that you should be based in Valencia in order for us to be in daily contact and ensure a smooth hand-over of leadership. I will expect you and your wife to spend the first year of your marriage living here at the Casillas mansion. If you return to your home in England it might lead to rumours of a rift between us, which would worry the board and our shareholders, who already have reservations about your suitability to head the company.'

The old man was as wily as a fox, Rafael thought furiously. 'I am certain that Juliet will not want to stay here after the vile way you spoke to her. Her daughter is settled at my home in London and it would not be good for the child to be brought to live in a different country.'

'Children are adaptable,' Hector said coolly. His black eyes bored into Rafael. 'Either you remain married for a year, or Lionel and his legal team will convince a court of law that your marriage is a fraudulent exercise intended to dupe me into appointing you as CEO.'

Rafael swore savagely. 'You cannot dictate where I choose to live or how I conduct my marriage.'

But he would not give his grandfather the satisfaction of seeing him lose his temper, and he swung round and strode out of the study. The truth was that the old man could do whatever he liked. Hector had won this round in their battle of wills, but he would not win the war. Whatever it took, he *would* claim his birthright, Rafael vowed.

\* \* \*

An hour on the treadmill relieved some of his tension, but he was still in a black rage when he left the gym and returned to his private suite of rooms. He headed straight to the bar and took a beer from the fridge. He could do with something stronger, but spending the afternoon getting drunk on Orujo—a fiercely strong spirit sometimes referred to as Spanish firewater—would not be a good idea. Especially as he was expected to attend a family lunch later with his wife.

*His wife.*

Rafael swore under his breath as he stepped outside onto the balcony which ran along the entire length of his apartment at the back of the mansion and overlooked the extensive gardens. In the distance the swimming pool glinted in the sunshine, but he wasn't interested in the view. His attention was fixed on Juliet.

She was standing a little way along the balcony, leaning against the stone balustrade. He knew it must be her, but his brain could not believe what his eyes were seeing. Gone were the saggy grey pyjamas and instead she was wearing an ivory-coloured silk chemise that skimmed her slender body. Her hair was even more of a surprise. Freed from the tight braid she usually wore, it reached almost to her waist and was not a dull brown, as Rafael had thought, but red-gold, gleaming like silk in the sunshine.

She was unaware of him and he stood and stared at her, not daring to move in case she was an illusion that might disappear if he alerted her to his presence. He was stunned to realise that the unflattering clothes he had always seen her wearing had hidden a slender but definitely feminine figure, with graceful lines and delicate curves.

As Rafael watched Juliet tilted her face up to the sun and lifted her arms above her head, stretching like a sleepy kitten. The gentle breeze flattened the silk chemise against her body, drawing his gaze to her small, high breasts. He could see the faint outline of her nipples, and heat rushed to his groin as he imagined sliding the straps of the chemise down her arms and peeling the silky material away from her breasts.

He cursed silently when he felt his arousal press against the thin material of his running shorts. *What the hell was happening to him?* Discovering that his mousy little wife might be more appealing than his initial opinion of her had suggested was not something he had ever anticipated.

Nor had he anticipated that his grandfather would react the way he had, Rafael thought grimly. He'd guessed Hector would be annoyed that he had not chosen a bride from the Spanish aristocracy, but he'd never imagined that the old man would break their agreement and refuse to appoint him CEO.

Rafael did not know if Juliet had heard him sigh or if she'd sensed that she was no longer alone. She was still half turned away from him, but when she spun round he felt another jolt of shock when he saw how her features were softened by the hair now framing her face. Her high cheekbones and almond-shaped eyes gave her a fey prettiness.

Now that he was really looking at her—rather than flicking an uninterested gaze over her—he noticed that her mouth was a little too wide for her heart-shaped face and the sweet curve of her lips was unexpectedly sensual.

He walked across the balcony, and as he

came nearer to her he saw the rosy flush on her face spread down her throat and across her décolletage. Her eyes widened, the pupils dilating. These subtle signals her body was sending out betrayed her awareness of him—which might work in his favour in light of the news he was about to break to her, he brooded.

Juliet watched Rafael saunter towards her and the wariness she felt for this stranger who was her husband was muddled with other confusing emotions that evoked a dragging sensation low in her pelvis.

It wasn't fair that he was so gorgeous, she thought ruefully. It had been difficult enough to keep her eyes off him when he'd been wearing a suit, or jeans and the navy polo shirt that he'd worn earlier when she had found him in the nursery with Poppy.

Now he must have come from the gym, and his black shorts and matching vest top revealed his powerfully muscular physique. His legs and arms were tanned a deep bronze, and she wondered if the sprinkling of black hair visible above his gym vest covered the whole of his chest.

She hated her reaction to his smouldering sensuality, very aware that he did not find her remotely attractive. But it was odd that he was staring at her intently, almost as if he had never seen her before. When she glanced down at the silk chemise she understood the reason for his scrutiny.

'Your sister lent me a nightdress because my pyjamas have been sent to the laundry,' she explained. 'I should have them back later today.'

'I do hope not,' Rafael said drily.

She grimaced, thinking of her pyjamas, which were as old and cheaply made as everything else she owned. After paying the bills and the monthly repayments on the money she'd borrowed from a loan company which charged a high interest rate, she used any spare cash to buy clothes for Poppy.

'It hardly matters to you that I have horrible pyjamas,' she said defensively. 'You won't see me wearing them. It's not as if we will have to spend any time together, or so you assured me.'

'I only meant that the temperature here in Valencia is much warmer than in England and you won't need to wear thick pyjamas to sleep in.'

'No, you didn't. You think I look terrible

and so do your family—apart from your sister, who is very kind.'

Juliet was grateful to Sofia for taking Poppy to play in a summerhouse in the garden with her twin daughters. Sofia had explained that she was married to an Englishman—Marcus Davenport. Her husband worked for a bank in Valencia and the family lived at the Casillas mansion. The twins had been brought up to be bilingual and happily chatted away to Poppy in English.

'I don't care what you or your relatives think of me. I have never pretended to be anything other than a working class single mother—which is precisely why you chose me for your bride,' Juliet reminded Rafael sharply, desperate to hide the hurt she felt.

She was quite aware that he had married her because he needed a wife, but it was humiliating to realise that he'd picked the most disgusting woman he could find so that he could antagonise his grandfather.

He exhaled heavily. 'I'm sorry that I subjected you to my grandfather's temper. Hector is angry with me, not you, but I should have considered your feelings when I involved you in my conflict with him.'

She bit her lip. Rafael's apology had sounded genuine but it did not change the situation. 'I don't want to stay here when it is patently obvious that Poppy and I are not welcome. It don't suppose your grandfather will want me to attend his birthday party. You said that he would make you CEO if you were married by the time of his birthday, and presumably that will still happen. There is no reason for me to stick around and I'm sure you will be relieved when I go.'

'I'm afraid you won't be going anywhere for a while,' Rafael said smoothly. 'For a year, in fact.'

'What do you mean?'

A frisson of unease ran the length of Juliet's spine as she stared at his hard face. He was so beautiful that just looking at him made her insides melt. But she had already experienced his ruthlessness and she did not trust him.

'Hector is refusing to make me CEO because he believes that our marriage is not genuine.'

'Well, that's that, then. Your plan has backfired.'

'Not entirely. On Saturday my grandfather will name me as his successor, and in a year's time he will stand down as head of the company as long as I am still married.' While Juliet was digesting this information, he continued. 'All we have to do is prove that our marriage is the real thing for a year.'

'No way.' She shook her head. 'Our agreement was that we would separate after a couple of months and divorce as soon as legally possible.'

'The contract you signed states that you will receive your money when I become CEO,' he reminded her.

'Then I'll forfeit the money.' She should have known it was too good to be true. 'I should never have agreed to a fake marriage. I just want to take Poppy back to England and forget that I ever met you.'

Rafael's eyes narrowed. 'Five million pounds for a year of your life doesn't sound unreasonable. The deal will be the same, except that you will live here at the Casillas mansion rather than at Ferndown House.'

'With one major difference. You said you wouldn't visit your home in Hampstead very often, but you're asking me to share your family's home in Spain with you. Even though the mansion is huge, we won't be able to avoid each other completely.'

'That's the point,' he said, in that sardonic way of his which made Juliet feel small and insignificant in the grand scheme of his determination to be CEO of his family's business. 'We'll have to live together to show my grandfather that our marriage is real.'

'But it isn't...' she whispered.

An image flashed into her mind of her parents, who had celebrated their wedding anniversary a few weeks before they were killed. Her mum had baked a cake in the shape of a heart, and her dad had gone to his allotment before dawn and come back with a huge bunch of colourful, fragrant sweetpeas which he'd left on the kitchen table next to a card addressed to his darling wife.

Her parents hadn't needed money to make them happy. Their love for each other and for her had been more precious than gold, Juliet thought, blinking away her tears before Rafael saw them.

'It doesn't make sense that your grandfather

is insisting on you staying married to me when he doesn't approve of me and knows that I am not the kind of woman you're attracted to,' she muttered.

Rafael's expression was inscrutable, but Juliet was mortified as the truth dawned on her.

'Hector thinks that you won't be able to bear being married to me for a whole year, doesn't he?'

'He is mistaken. I will do whatever I have to,' he said grimly.

'*You* might be willing to lie back and think… not of England, in this case, but of the CEO-ship that you'll gain from being married to the Bride of Frankenstein,' Juliet snapped, 'but I won't do it. You can't force me to stay.'

'You're being melodramatic.' Rafael sounded amused. 'I can't force you to remain in our marriage, it's true. But I suggest you think about what you stand to lose if you walk away now. You told me that your daughter's father wants custody of her and will try to prove that you are unfit to have Poppy living with you. It's hard to see how a judge would back your claim over your ex's if you were homeless or placed in a hostel by social services.'

Juliet swallowed hard, knowing that Rafael was right. 'However,' he continued, 'you are my wife, and Poppy is my stepdaughter, and I will ensure that you have the support of my best legal team. I think it is likely that a family court will look favourably on the fact that Poppy is living in a comfortable home in a secure family unit and she will be allowed to remain with her mother.'

She couldn't argue with Rafael's logical assessment of the situation, Juliet acknowledged despairingly. He had said he would do whatever it took to get what he wanted and she understood that, because she would walk over hot coals to keep Poppy.

'If your grandfather suspects that you've tried to trick him how can we convince him that our marriage is not fake? No one will believe that you fell for someone like me.' When his brows lifted, she said crossly, 'You've dated some of the most beautiful women in the world and you are frequently photographed by the paparazzi with a supermodel or a famous actress draped around you. I'm under no illusions about the way I look. I've always been thin, and I was clearly in the wrong queue when breasts were given out...'

He laughed, and it was so unexpected that Juliet stared at him, mesmerised by the way his lips curved upwards at the corners.

'You're funny,' he said, and there was faint surprise in his voice, as if he had discovered something unexpected about her. He stretched out his hand and touched her hair. 'I see now where your daughter gets her strawberry blonde hair from.'

Suddenly it was hard to speak because her mouth had gone dry. 'Poppy's hair is much fairer than mine,' she muttered.

'Your hair is the colour of amber. It suits you when you leave it loose.'

'After a shower I came to sit outside, so that my hair would dry in the sunshine. Usually I keep it tied up, because it gets in the way when I'm playing with Poppy...'

Juliet knew she was waffling, to distract herself from suddenly finding that Rafael was much closer. How had he moved without her noticing?

He was so much taller than her and she found herself staring at the ridges of his impressive pectoral muscles visible through his tight-fitting sports vest. The scent of him—spicy cologne, sweat, *male*—assailed her senses. She tilted her head so that she could see his face and her heart missed a beat when she discovered that he was looking at her intently. The gleam in his olive-green eyes startled her, and she told herself she must be imagining the very male interest in gaze.

Rafael wasn't interested in her as a woman. To him she was merely a tool to help him get what he wanted, she reminded herself.

She backed away from him but found herself trapped between his partially clothed muscle-packed body and the wall of the balcony. He placed his hands flat on the top of the balustrade on either side of her and frowned when she shrank from him.

'We are going to have trouble convincing my grandfather that our marriage was made in heaven if you flinch every time I come near you,' he said impatiently. 'You did the same thing during our wedding.'

'You didn't warn me before the ceremony that you would kiss me, and I wasn't expecting it.'

He gave her a sardonic look, but slowly the expression in his eyes changed to something else—something hot that caused Juliet's heart-rate to quicken. 'In that case I'm giving you fair warning that it will be necessary for us to kiss whenever any of my relatives are around and we are on show, so to speak.'

Her tongue darted out to moisten her dry lips. 'You don't want to kiss me...' She would never forget his appalled expression when he had seen her in the mustard-coloured dress she had worn for their wedding.

'I'm coming round to the idea,' he drawled. 'And by the way, I don't think you look like the Bride of Frankenstein.'

'I'm flattered.' She tried to sound sarcastic but her voice was a thread of sound.

Her breath hitched in her throat when Rafael bent his head towards her so that he blotted out the sun. He was so gorgeous, and it would be so easy to fall under his magnetic spell, but it would be dangerous.

She turned her face away and felt his warm breath graze her cheek. 'I don't want you to kiss me.'

He captured her chin between his long fingers and exerted gentle pressure so that she was forced to look at him. 'How do you know until you've tried it? You might enjoy it.'

That was what she was afraid of.

She could not hide the tremor that ran through her when he dragged his thumb pad over her bottom lip.

'You are not my prisoner, and I am not doing anything to prevent you from going back inside the house,' Rafael murmured. 'But if you don't move in the next ten seconds I *am* going to kiss you.'

It was true that she could easily step past him. But her feet seemed to be cemented to the floor. Her instinct for self-protection urged her to run, but a stronger instinct that was deeply rooted in her womanhood held her there against the balustrade as Rafael's mouth came nearer.

Her heart was beating at three times its normal rate and he placed his finger over the pulse that was going crazy at the base of her throat. And then he brushed his lips across hers and the world tilted on its axis.

She had expected him to kiss her with the bold arrogance that was integral to him, but his mouth was gentle on hers, warm and seductive, disarming her defences so that her lips parted without her volition. Even then he kept it light, undemanding, tasting her with little sips that teased and tantalised so that she pressed her body closer to his and placed her hands flat on his chest.

Juliet felt the powerful thud of his heart beneath her fingertips and with a little sigh of capitulation kissed him back. Her eyelashes swept down and her senses became attuned to the taste of him on her lips, the warmth of his breath filling her mouth and the evocative masculine scent that wrapped around her as she melted, soft and pliant, against his whipcord body.

# CHAPTER FIVE

'THAT WASN'T SO difficult, was it?'

Rafael's voice broke through the sensual haze that had wrapped around Juliet and she blinked at him, half blinded by the bright sunshine in her eyes as he lifted his head and she was no longer in his shadow. She wondered why he had stopped kissing her, but then reality hit and she remembered he had been demonstrating how they would have to act in public to convince his grandfather that their marriage was genuine.

And she had just demonstrated to Rafael that she couldn't resist him!

Following his gaze, she glanced down and a fresh wave of embarrassment swept over her when she saw the outline of her pebble-hard nipples beneath the silk chemise. She looked back at him, expecting to see mockery in his eyes, but he seemed unusually tense, and it was obvious that he couldn't wait to get away from her when he swung round and strode across the balcony.

He paused as he reached the bi-fold glass doors. 'The nurse said that your temperature has returned to normal and you are feeling much better?' When Juliet nodded, he continued, 'We are expected to attend a family lunch later, so that you can meet more of my relatives.'

She thought of the sea of faces that had stared at her as if she had been beamed down from Mars when Rafael had brought her to the Casillas mansion. 'You mean there are *more*?'

'My grandfather is the oldest of seven siblings, and there are numerous uncles, aunts and cousins, many of whom work within the company and have an opinion on who they think should succeed Hector. Some of them support me—rather more of them don't,' he said sardonically.

It sounded like a family at war. Juliet bit her lip. 'I'd rather not be subjected to further humiliation and I don't want to risk Poppy being upset again. Can't you say that I am still unwell?'

'My grandfather will expect us to be at the

lunch and it will be an opportunity to show him that we are a couple who are in love.'

Juliet wondered why his words evoked an ache in her heart. She had never been in love. Her crush on Bryan had ended abruptly when he'd brutally told her she had been a one-night stand. And Rafael had warned her not to fall in love with him. But now he was asking her to pretend that he was the man of her dreams.

'I'm not that good an actress,' she muttered.

'I thought your performance a few moments ago was very convincing—unless it wasn't an act and you actually *enjoyed* kissing me?' he said silkily.

While Juliet was searching her mind for a clever retort, he spoke again.

'Sofia's twins will have their lunch in the nursery with the nanny—Poppy might be happier staying with them.'

He had kissed Juliet to show her how they would have to act like happy newlyweds in front of his grandfather. That was the *only* reason, Rafael assured himself. Although perhaps there had been an element of curiosity too, he conceded.

The realisation that he had been too hasty when he'd dismissed his wife as being plain and unattractive had stirred his interest. But he had been unprepared for his reaction to the feel of her soft lips beneath his. Quite simply he had been blown away by the sweet sensuality of Juliet's response, and his gut had clenched when she had kissed him with an intriguing mix of innocence and desire.

*Dios*, there had been a moment when his cool logic had almost been superseded by fiery passion, and he'd been on the verge of deepening the kiss and drawing her slender figure up close against his hard body. Fortunately he had remembered in time that it would be a mistake to become involved with her. Juliet was more vulnerable than he had thought when he'd suggested their marriage deal.

*Face it*, Rafael told himself grimly, you didn't think about *her* at all.

She was simply a means by which he could achieve his goal of becoming CEO, and nothing in that respect had changed—except that out there on the balcony it had fleetingly crossed his mind that he would like to have sex with her. But that would further complicate an already complicated situation, he brooded as he slid his arms into his suit jacket.

Rafael's private apartment in the mansion consisted of an open-plan lounge-cum-dining room, a kitchen and his study. There was also a large master bedroom, with his-and-hers dressing rooms and en suite bathrooms. He had asked the staff to put a single bed in Juliet's dressing room, so that Poppy could sleep near to her mother, and he had been sleeping on the sofa in his dressing room, leaving the bed for Juliet while she was ill.

There would have to be a change to the sleeping arrangements, he decided. He was six foot three, and he couldn't spend every night for the next year with his feet hanging off the end of a sofa.

Pushing open the bedroom door, he stifled a sigh when he saw Juliet. It had suited him that she looked like a drab waif when he'd wanted to annoy his grandfather with his unsuitable bride. Now there had been a change of plan, but unfortunately Juliet's dress sense had not improved.

Her outfit of a denim skirt with a frayed hem and a flamingo-pink jumper that clashed with her reddish hair was only marginally less un-flattering than the abomination of a dress she had been wearing when he had introduced her to his family two days ago.

'I should have mentioned that lunch will be a formal affair,' he said.

At least she had made a bit of effort with her hair, and it was piled on top of her head in a neat bun. The style showed off the elegant line of her throat, but inexplicably Rafael wished she had left her hair loose so that he could run his fingers through it.

Her face was no longer unhealthily pale. Spending some time outside in the sunshine had put a pink flush on her cheeks. He would have to make sure that she wore sunscreen, he thought. Her English rose complexion would burn easily.

She shrugged. 'I don't own any designer clothes. There wasn't any need for them at my cleaning job,' she told him drily.

He strode into her dressing room and opened the wardrobe door, grimacing when it was immediately obvious that she had spoken the truth. 'You *must* own other footwear besides those things,' he muttered, looking at her scuffed winter boots.

Instead of replying she took a pair of tatty trainers out of the wardrobe and waved them in front of him. 'You married me precisely because my clothes look like they came from a jumble sale. Frankly, your plan to try and convince your grandfather that you've married your fantasy woman is just not going to work.'

'We both have a vested interest in *making* it work,' he reminded her. 'And we will have a better chance if you are a little less lippy.'

Against his will his gaze was drawn to her mouth, and he remembered how her lips had parted beneath his, so soft and moist and willing. He'd sensed her disappointment when he'd ended the kiss. Beneath her belligerent attitude she was attracted to him. But it would not be fair to lead her on or let her believe that he could fulfil any romantic notions she might have about him.

'I will arrange an appointment for you with a personal stylist who can advise you on what clothes will suit your figure instead of swamping you,' he said abruptly. He glanced at his watch. 'We had better go downstairs. Lunch is in ten minutes.'

He escorted Juliet out of his private suite, and as they descended the grand staircase and walked through the house he had to wait several times while she stopped to admire the artwork on the walls.

'Don't tell me that's an original Van Gogh?' she said, sounding amazed. 'And a Cezanne and a Renoir? It's an impressive art collection. Do the paintings belong to your grandfather?'

'Some of them are mine. I bought the Jackson Pollock at auction a year ago.'

He was curious about where a girl from a council estate who sold sandwiches and cleaned for a living had gained such an in-depth knowledge of art. Juliet intrigued him... Rafael frowned as he admitted to himself that she was the only woman ever to have done so.

She stood in front of the Pollock and studied the painting. 'It looks like the artist just threw paint at the canvas. I don't like it. Do you?'

He shrugged. 'I've never thought about whether I like it or not. I paid one hundred and twenty million dollars for the painting, which I bought as an investment.'

She tilted her head to one side and studied him thoughtfully, the same way she had looked at the painting. 'Fancy paying all that money for something that doesn't fill your heart with joy.'

'I will be paying a lot of money for *you*, but I am not feeling joy right now, *chiquita*. I'm feeling exasperated,' he growled. He glanced at her, clumping along next to him in her scuffed boots, and sighed. 'I had forgotten that you haven't had a chance to look around the house because your illness has confined you to bed. I'll give you a tour after lunch.'

He was about to open the dining room door but Juliet put her hand on his arm. 'Is it going to be as awful as last time?' she said in a low tone.

Why hadn't he thought that she would be nervous about meeting his family again— especially his grandfather? And who could blame her? Guilt snaked through Rafael at knowing he had put Juliet in this situation.

Her eyes were huge in her face and her small hand was cold when he wrapped his fingers around hers. 'I have explained that Hector is not angry with *you*.'

'He's disappointed with me because I'm not good enough to be your wife.'

He grimaced. 'No, *cariño*. My grandfather has always been disappointed with *me*. You have done nothing wrong and I won't allow him to insult you again.'

Despite Rafael's reassurance, Juliet felt sick with nerves when he ushered her into the dining room and led her over to the group of people who were gathered by the open French doors where pre-lunch drinks were being served.

He introduced her to his numerous relatives and she was conscious of the curious glances they gave her.

Worse were the unflattering comments she overheard his mother make about her clothes. Perhaps Rafael had not informed his family that she understood Spanish.

The tangible antagonism between him and his mother, the icily elegant Delfina Casillas, was another puzzle. She remembered that Rafael had mentioned he had a stepbrother, but he didn't seem to be at the lunch.

When they sat down for the meal she was relieved that Hector was seated at the far end of the table. He did not pay her any attention, but she was too on edge to enjoy the five courses, and she opted for water rather than wine so that she kept a clear head. She was toying with her dessert—a chocolate confection that at any other time she would have adored—when Hector spoke to her in English.

'Rafael tells me that you ran your own business in London. What type of business?'

Conversation around the table suddenly stopped and Juliet sensed that everyone was looking at her. She lifted her chin. 'I sold sandwiches and delivered them to office staff at lunchtimes.'

'You worked in catering?'

Hector's tone was as scathing as if she'd announced that she had worked as a stripper. Her temper simmered. She hated snobbery, and having been subjected to it at ballet school by some of the other pupils she had learned to stand up for herself.

'Yes. I also had a cleaning job in the evenings—pushing an industrial floor-polishing machine around a shopping centre.'

'*Santa Madre! Ella es un domestico!*' the old

man muttered to Rafael's mother, who was sitting next to him.

Delfina's expression became even haughtier as she glanced along the table at Juliet.

'Abuelo, there is no need for you to be rude about my wife,' Rafael said curtly.

Juliet's heart lifted at his defence of her—until she remembered that he was determined to convince his grandfather he was in love with her.

She looked over at Hector. 'Presumably you are unaware that I speak Spanish and that I can understand the horrible things you have said about me? I am not from the gutter. My parents weren't wealthy but they were hard-working, and they taught me good manners—which you seem to lack.'

A gasp went around the table, and beside her she felt Rafael stiffen, but she was too angry to care.

'And there is no shame in doing domestic work. Without the staff who run this house you would have to clean your own floors.'

As quickly as her temper had flared it cooled again, and she wished she was anywhere but sitting at this table, with Hector Casillas looking at her disdainfully as if she were a piece of rubbish. What if he decided not to appoint Rafael CEO because she had allowed her pride to get the better of her? She did not dare glance at Rafael, certain that he must be furious with her, and she was startled when he gave a shout of laughter.

'Well said, *querida*.' He looked over at his grandfather. 'As you have just discovered, Abuelo, my wife is petite in stature but she is as fierce as a lioness.'

Juliet turned her head towards her husband and her heart lurched when he smiled at her, showing his even white teeth. She must have imagined that note of admiration in his voice, she told herself.

Following her outburst the atmosphere in the dining room among his relatives was strained and she could not wait for the meal to be over. It was Sofia who broke the awkward silence.

'Where did you learn to speak Spanish, Juliet?'

'My aunt is married to a Spaniard and Uncle Carlos insisted on speaking Spanish at home with Aunt Vivian and my cousins. I lived with them for a couple of years, and quickly picked up on how to speak the language, but I'm not confident at reading and writing in Spanish.'

It was for that reason she had been unable to find a better paid job as a translator, Juliet thought ruefully.

'Did you live in Spain with your aunt and uncle?' Sofia asked.

'No—Australia. They settled in Sydney twenty years ago, but my uncle wanted to feel a connection to his birth country.'

'What about your parents? Do they also live in Australia?'

She shook her head. 'Mum and Dad died before Poppy was born.'

'I'm so sorry,' Sofia said gently. 'I assume your parents were not very old. Did they lose their lives in an accident?'

'Their car broke down on a motorway and they were waiting for the rescue truck. It was a foggy night and a lorry ploughed into them. They were both killed instantly.'

'What a terrible tragedy. You must have been devastated.'

'Yes.'

Memories flooded Juliet's mind of the night that her life had been blown apart. She missed her parents so much and she felt very alone—an outsider in Rafael's family home, made to feel unwelcome by his relatives. Tears blurred her eyes and she stared down at the table while she struggled to bring her emotions under control. To her horror she felt a tear slide down her cheek and drip onto the tablecloth. The bead of moisture darkened the pristine white cloth as it soaked into the material.

Rafael made a low sound in his throat, almost like a groan, and placed his hand over hers, where she was resting it on the table. That human connection—the warmth of his skin as he threaded his fingers through hers—tugged on her heart.

For a few moments she allowed herself to daydream that he actually cared about her as he lifted her hand to his mouth and pressed his lips against her knuckles. Her eyes flew to his and he held her gaze, his expression softer than she had ever seen it. Time seemed to be suspended, and it was as if there were only the two of them floating in a private universe.

Juliet released a shaky breath—but when she glanced around the table she saw that Hector was watching them and understanding dawned. Rafael was acting in front of his grandfather and she was a fool for wishing that his concern was genuine.

When the lunch was over, and they stood up and walked out of the dining room, she tried to snatch her hand out of his. 'Hector can't see us now, so you can stop pretending to be sympathetic,' she muttered.

'I wasn't pretending.' He stopped walking and stared down at her, tightening his fingers around her hand so that she could not pull free. 'I am not without compassion. You have been through a hell of a lot.'

She shook her head, refusing to allow herself to fall for the huskiness in his voice. 'Like you *care*, Rafael,' she said sarcastically. 'I realise that for the next year I will have to act like your loving wife in public, but I don't want your pseudo-sympathy or your fake kisses.'

Something indecipherable flared in his eyes. 'There was nothing fake about the chemistry we both felt this morning or the way you responded when I kissed you. Perhaps I should remind you?'

Without being aware of how she'd got there, Juliet found herself standing in a small alcove off the marble-lined entrance hall. Rafael ignored her renewed attempts to free her hand by the simple method of repositioning it behind her back.

He swore when she kicked his shin. 'Calm down, you little wildcat.'

She glared at him, her heart thudding unevenly as he lowered his head. 'I don't want you to kiss me.'

'We've been through that once.'

He sounded bored, but his eyes glittered with something that Juliet was stunned to realise was desire. For *her*. He lifted his other hand and pulled the pins out of her bun, so that her hair unravelled and spilled over her shoulders.

'No one is around to see us so why are you doing this?' she asked desperately.

'You need to practise kissing,' he told her.

His voice was deadpan, but there was a wicked gleam in his eyes that made her stomach swoop.

'It's my guess that you haven't had much experience.'

'I'm sorry if you were disappointed by my efforts earlier,' she choked. 'Do you take pleasure in humiliating me?'

'I find this much more pleasurable,' he murmured against her lips, his breath mingling with hers as he brought his mouth down and kissed her with a possessiveness that decimated her defences.

And Juliet surrendered. She suspected that she would hate herself later, but right now she was powerless to fight the restless longing that stirred low in her belly as Rafael deepened the kiss and explored the shape of her lips with his tongue before he dipped it into her mouth, demanding a response that she could not deny him.

She had never felt like this before—wild and hungry and aching with a passion that stung her nipples and tugged sharp and needy between her thighs. Rafael had been right to think that she hadn't had much experience of kissing or anything else.

She'd only been on a few dates with Bryan before he had suggested they spend the night together. Naively she'd believed that he was in love with her, as she had been with him, and so she had agreed.

Her first and only sexual experience had been uncomfortable and unsatisfactory—

which he had assured her was *her* fault. Bryan had not wanted her for more than one night—and Rafael did not want her at all. Not really.

He had married her because she was unattractive and now he was stuck with her for a year. He couldn't resume his playboy lifestyle while he had to convince his grandfather that his marriage was genuine. Faced with a choice of celibacy or sex with his wife, perhaps he had decided that she was the better of the two options.

Shame doused the fire inside her and she jerked her mouth away from his. 'No.'

'*No?*' He sounded as dazed as she felt and he was breathing hard. 'I could very easily persuade you to retract that statement, *chiquita...*' he rasped.

'Why would you want to? We both know that I am the last woman you would desire. I am too thin and plain.' She bit her lip. 'I've seen pictures of the supermodels you take to bed.'

His eyes narrowed. 'You are not plain. You just need the right clothes for your shape.'

'My mother used to say that you can't make a silk purse out of a sow's ear. I know what I am, and more to the point I know my lack of looks and sophistication are the reasons you married me.'

It hurt more than it should, and she pushed past him, hating the idea that he might pity her.

She ran up the grand staircase and then hesitated on the landing when she realised that she had no idea where Rafael's suite of rooms were or, more importantly, the location of the nursery. Her arms ached to hold her daughter and feel the unconditional love that Poppy gave her and she returned a thousandfold.

'Are you lost?' Rafael's sister walked along the corridor towards her and laughed when Juliet nodded. 'The house is huge, isn't it? When Rafael and I first came to live here we couldn't get over how grand it is.'

'I assumed you were both born here. Where did you live before you moved into the mansion?'

Sofia gave her a thoughtful look. 'You should ask my brother. Here's the nursery.' She seemed relieved to change the subject. 'I promised to take the twins swimming this afternoon. Will you and Poppy join us?'

'Neither of us have swimwear. I've never taken Poppy swimming. The local pool where we lived in London was closed down by the council. There was a pool at a private gym but I couldn't afford the membership fees.' Juliet flushed and looked away from Rafael's elegant sister.

'I'm sure you have always done your best for your daughter,' Sofia said gently. 'But Poppy can use one of the swimsuits that the girls have grown out of, and I'll lend you a swimming costume.'

Juliet's conscience would not allow Poppy to miss out on her first experience of swimming, and the little girl's excitement when they arrived at the pool later that afternoon helped her to overcome her reluctance to slip off the towelling robe and reveal the sky-blue swimsuit that Sofia had lent her.

The twins were already in the water and Juliet noted that they were proficient swimmers. She felt guilty that her circumstances meant that Poppy had missed out on so many things—especially a father, she thought as she watched Sofia's husband playing with his daughters. He waded up the steps carrying Ana and Inez in each arm, and Sofia introduced him to Juliet.

'I was meant to arrive back in time for lunch but my flight was delayed,' Marcus Davenport explained. His pleasant face broke into a grin. 'I hear that you stood up to Hector? I wish I had been there to witness it.'

Sofia and Marcus were so friendly that Juliet started to relax as she played in the pool with Poppy, who was wearing armbands and bobbing about happily in the water.

'There's an indoor pool too, and Poppy will soon learn to swim without water aids if you bring her every day,' Sofia said.

For the first time since Rafael had dropped the bombshell that they would have to remain married for a year and live at the Casillas mansion Juliet realised that there would be some benefits—especially for her daughter. Poppy was already picking up a few Spanish words from the twins, and she would have so much freedom to play in the gardens or at the beach, which had been visible when Juliet had stood on the balcony that morning.

Her stomach hollowed as she remembered what had happened when Rafael had found her on the balcony. He had kissed her, and it had been so much better than she'd imagined.

And she had imagined it often.

Her secret fantasies, in which he swept her into his arms and claimed her mouth with his, had not been disappointed by the sensual expertise of his kiss. Just thinking about it made her breasts tingle, and when she glanced down she was dismayed to see the hard points of her nipples outlined beneath her swimsuit.

The sound of a familiar gravelly voice with a sexy accent caused her to spin round, and she quickly ducked her shoulders under the water when she saw Rafael standing at the edge of the pool. A pair of navy blue swim shorts sat low on his hips, and Juliet's gaze skittered over his hair-roughened thighs before moving up to his flat abdomen and broad, tanned chest covered in silky black hair.

*Oh, my!* She edged into deeper water to hide her body's reaction to his rampant masculinity.

Poppy gave a squeal of delight when she saw Rafael. 'Raf—are you coming swimming?'

'Would you like me to, *conejita*?'

He swung himself down into the pool and dived below the surface before reappearing and raking his wet hair off his brow with his hands.

'Let me see you swim, little rabbit,' he said to Poppy, and she immediately kicked her feet the way Juliet had tried to persuade her to do for the past twenty minutes.

They stayed in the water for a while longer, until Poppy started to shiver, and then Rafael lifted her onto the poolside where Elvira was waiting with a towel. He turned back to Juliet and frowned when he saw her tense expression. 'What's the matter? We are meant to be playing happy families but you haven't stopped glaring at me.'

'That's just it. This is a game to you,' she said tautly. 'But while you are *"playing happy families"* to impress your grandfather, there is a danger that Poppy will become fond of you. When I agreed to our marriage deal it was only going to be for a couple of months, but now we have to stay together for a year and it will be harder on Poppy when I take her back to England.'

'Are you saying that I should *ignore* your daughter?' Rafael's frown deepened. 'I realise the situation has changed and I won't suddenly drop out of Poppy's life in a year's time.' He swore beneath his breath when Juliet gave him a disbelieving look. 'It is not my intention to upset Poppy. She is a delightful child and a credit to you,' he said gruffly.

'She likes you,' Juliet muttered. 'You are good with her and your nieces.'

The truth was that she'd felt a tug of jealousy when Poppy had wanted to play with Rafael rather than with her. She had been surprised that he was so patient with her daughter and his sister's little girls.

'You'll make a good father when you have children of your own.'

'That's never going to happen.' His tone dropped several degrees. 'I've no desire to have children.'

'What if your wife wants a family? I don't mean me,' she added hastily. 'But in the future you might meet the right woman and fall in love with her.'

'I told you when you agreed to be my wife that I do not believe in love.' He walked up the steps out of the pool and grabbed a towel from a nearby sunbed. 'Lust is an emotion I understand, but that doesn't last for ever. Unfortunately too many people only discover that after they have made a legal commitment to spend the rest of their lives together, and the only winners are the divorce lawyers.'

'Why are you so cynical? My parents were as much in love with each other when they died as they were on the day they married. They were happy together for more than twenty years.' She swallowed. 'It might sound odd, but I'm glad they were together when they were killed. I don't know how one would have survived without the other.'

Juliet followed Rafael out of the pool and stopped dead when she saw him staring at her leg. She had been so engrossed in their conversation that she'd forgotten about the scar that ran from the top of her thigh to just above her knee. The scar had faded over the years, but she was chilly after being in the pool and it was now a vivid purple welt on her pale skin.

Avoiding his gaze, she hurried over to where she had left her robe and wrapped it around her, thankful that it covered her leg. She had come to terms with the scar, or so she'd thought, but she wished Rafael hadn't seen it. No doubt now he thought she was ugly as well as plain.

'What happened to you?' he asked quietly.

'I was in my parents' car when the lorry crashed into the back of it.'

'*Dios.*' He dropped his towel and strode over to her, settling his hand on her shoulder. 'I didn't realise that you were with your parents when they died.'

'I don't remember much about the accident.' Juliet automatically turned her head to check on Poppy, and saw her playing in a sandpit with the twins. 'The car developed a problem while we were driving along the motorway and my dad pulled over onto the hard shoulder. It was winter and very foggy. I was sitting in the front passenger seat and Dad told me to stay there while he went to get my coat out of the boot. Mum got out with him, and that's when the lorry smashed into us.'

She was conscious of Rafael curling his fingers tighter around her shoulder. She had never really spoken about what had happened to anyone before, but now the words came tumbling out.

'All I remember is a loud noise like an explosion. I was in a coma for two weeks, and when I came round I was told that my femur had been shattered by the impact of the crash.

At first the surgeon thought that my leg would have to be amputated, but he did everything he could and saved it. My thigh bone is held together with several metal pins.' She swallowed. 'My aunt had flown over from Australia and she broke the news about my parents when I came out of Intensive Care.'

*'Dios!'* Rafael repeated roughly. 'Has your leg healed fully?'

'It's fine now, but eighteen months ago I had to have some more surgery and I was in hospital for a few weeks. Aunt Viv couldn't come over from Australia then, because she was ill herself. There was no one to look after Poppy so she stayed with foster parents.'

Juliet felt a pang, remembering how desperately she had missed her daughter while they had been apart. She watched the sunlight glinting on the surface of the pool. It was so bright that it made her eyes sting. That was the reason for the tears that blurred her vision, she assured herself.

'Poppy is all I have,' she whispered. 'Bryan has never been interested in her but now he's threatening to take my baby away from me.' She spun away from Rafael and his hand fell from her shoulder. 'I won't let that happen,' she said fiercely. 'That's why I agreed to your marriage deal and why I am determined to see it through.'

She stared at his beautiful face, at the mouth that had wreaked such havoc on hers.

'I'm using you as much as you are using me. Let's hope that we both end up with what we want in a year's time.'

## CHAPTER SIX

RAFAEL STROLLED THROUGH the marble and gold entrance hall in the Casillas mansion, clearly designed to impress, with a champagne flute in one hand and a smile on his lips that anyone who knew him well—which only his sister did—would realise was entirely fake. He stopped to speak to his uncle, but although he was fond of Tio Alvaro, who was one of his supporters, Rafael's attention was on the grand staircase where he expected to see Juliet appear.

Where the hell *was* his wife?

When he had knocked on the door of her dressing room before he'd come down to greet the guests who were arriving for his grandfather's birthday party Sofia had called out that Juliet would be ready in ten minutes. That had been a quarter of an hour ago, and Rafael was growing concerned that she did not want to leave her room because she was afraid of being subjected to another frosty reception from certain members of his family.

He had barely seen her for the past two days, while he had been at work at the Casillas Group's head office in Valencia. He'd arranged for her to go shopping with a personal stylist who would advise her on a new wardrobe, and Sofia had offered to look after Poppy. However, Rafael had yet to see if the stylist had been successful in finding some clothes which suited Juliet's figure.

She had been fast asleep in his bed by the time he'd returned to the mansion late in the evenings, after long days of business meetings. And, aware that she had only recently recovered from the virus that had made her so unwell, he had been reluctant to disturb her and had slept on the sofa in his dressing room again.

But she had been on his mind a lot. Too much. Instead of concentrating on what was being said at the meetings he had found himself thinking of Juliet when they had been at the pool. He'd pictured her in that light blue swimsuit which matched the startling blue of her eyes. The clingy material had revealed her slender figure and small, round breasts. She was as fragile as a bird, and when he'd seen that scar on her leg, before she had quickly wrapped her robe around her to hide it from him, he'd been struck once again by her mix of vulnerability and incredible courage.

The realisation that Juliet might have died along with her parents in the car accident, and that he might never have met her, disturbed Rafael more than it should. After all, it was not as if she meant anything to him. He kept his affairs short and sweet, aware of the damage that the unstable mix of emotions and relation-ships could produce. His mother had followed her heart when she'd eloped with his father, and Rafael was the damaged product of his parents' messed-up lives.

'It is a big night for you tonight, eh?' said Tio Alvaro.

Rafael nodded his head, not entirely sure what his uncle meant.

'I have heard rumours that Hector is going to announce you as his successor. It is what you have wanted for a long time?'

'Ah, yes.'

Rafael did not explain that his grandfather's

announcement would contain a caveat and that the hand-over of power would not happen immediately. To his astonishment he realised that he had not given Hector's announcement a thought. He had waited for years and fought hard to claim his birthright, but tonight his mind was on Juliet rather than the CEO-ship.

He raked a hand through his hair and asked himself why he was allowing a slip of a girl with an understated sensuality and eyes that he could drown in to affect him. Something caught his attention, and when he looked up towards the top of the staircase he felt the new experience of his heart colliding painfully with his ribs.

*'Ah, querida...'* he murmured beneath his breath.

He had already been surprised by Juliet— by her unexpected fiery nature and the sensual heat of her kiss that had made him ache for hours afterwards. But as he watched her begin to descend the grand marble staircase, one hand holding lightly onto the banister rail, he was quite simply awestruck.

She shimmered. There was no other way to describe her. The effect was created by the hundreds of gold sequins that covered her ball gown, but there was something else that made Juliet sparkle. It was self-confidence and pride, Rafael thought as he strode across the hall to the base of the staircase. It was also, he mused as he stood there, unable to take his eyes off her, her own realisation that she was beautiful. So very beautiful.

And she was certainly making an entrance. The eyes of every person in the hall were focused on his stunning, sexy wife as she walked down the stairs towards him.

How had he not seen before how utterly lovely she was? Well-fitting clothes helped, of course. The gown had been designed to mould her slender frame and emphasise the narrowness of her waist. The bodice was strapless and her small breasts were displayed like perfect round peaches above the low-cut neckline. The shimmering gold material followed the gentle contours of her hips before finally flaring out trumpet style to the floor.

She seemed to glide down the stairs, and Rafael caught a glimpse of gold stiletto heels beneath the hem of her dress. He lifted his gaze up to her hair, which had had three or four inches cut off its length and now fell to mid-way down her back, gleaming like polished amber beneath the bright lights of the chandeliers. A stylist had added some wispy layers to the front sections of her hair, which framed her face and drew attention to her high cheekbones and forget-me-not-blue eyes.

When she halted two steps above where he was waiting for her Rafael saw that her fair eyebrows and lashes had been darkened with make-up and her mouth was coated in a rose-coloured gloss. The finishing touch to her transformation was her perfume—floral notes mixed with an edgier, more sensual fragrance that assailed his senses and evoked a kick of heat in his groin.

As he studied her he saw a wariness in her expression that he instantly wanted to banish. *'Bella,'* he murmured, capturing her hand in his and lifting it to his mouth. 'I'm speechless, *chiquita.* I would never have believed...

'That a sow's ear could be turned into something passably attractive?' she suggested.

'I never want to hear you use that terrible expression again. You are not and never have been a sow's ear.'

But he had been blind, Rafael acknowledged. Worse, he had been arrogant enough to believe that he could use Juliet to further his raging ambition. He had chosen her because of her downtrodden appearance. *Dios*, he had treated her as scornfully as his grandfather had. But Juliet's ethereal beauty hid an incredible strength of will. She was a survivor—as he was—and he knew how lonely that felt.

Shame ran through Rafael. Distaste for his presumption that Juliet's lack of money made her less worthy of his respect. He had spent the past twenty years fighting prejudice from his family because of his lowly background—part-*gitano*, born in the gutter to a drug-dealer father. But he had ruthlessly exploited Juliet's financial problems to persuade her to marry him without considering how humiliated she would feel to be despised by his rich relatives.

'You look exquisite,' he assured her. 'I take it that your shopping trip was a success?'

She caught her lower lip between her teeth, making him want to soothe the place with his tongue. 'The personal stylist insisted that I needed dozens of outfits to reflect my position as your wife. She spent a *fortune* on clothes.

But I'll pay you back when—' She broke off and glanced around to check that they could not be overheard by anyone. 'When our marriage deal ends.'

Rafael laid his finger lightly across her lips, refusing to question why he did not want to think of the motive behind their marriage. 'I believe in living for the moment,' he said softly. 'And at this moment, *querida*, I will be honoured to escort my beautiful wife into the ballroom.'

Juliet smiled and her elfin beauty made his gut clench. He drew her arm through his and walked her into the ballroom, where most of the three hundred guests were now assembled and waiters were serving champagne and canapés. Many of Spain's elite—a mix of old money aristocrats and nouveau riche millionaires—were on the guest list.

He took a glass of champagne offered by a waiter and gave it to Juliet before he took a glass for himself. *'Salud.'*

She sipped her drink. 'Is it real champagne? I've only ever had sparkling wine.'

'Of course it's real champagne. My grandfather would not allow fizzy wine to be served at his eightieth birthday party,' he said drily.

'It's lovely.' She took another sip and giggled. 'It feels like the bubbles are exploding on my tongue.'

Rafael stared at her. He could not stop himself. Juliet was like a breath of fresh air, and he realised how stultifying and predictable his life had become until she had burst into it.

He did not know what to make of the feelings she stirred in him. The hot rush of desire that went straight to his groin was something he understood, but he felt possessive, protective, and a host of other emotions that had never troubled him before.

Juliet bit her lip and he realised that she had mistaken his brooding silence for irritation. 'I'm not sophisticated,' she mumbled, rosy colour running under her skin.

'Thank God,' he reassured her.

The band had started playing and he led her over to the dance floor, handing their empty glasses to a waiter before he drew her into his arms. Even in high heels she was so much smaller than him that he could rest his chin on the top of her head.

She danced with a natural grace that captivated him, and he swore silently when he felt the predictable reaction of a certain part of his anatomy to the sensation of Juliet's lithe body pressed up against his hard thighs. He was in trouble, Rafael acknowledged, seizing the excuse that the tune had finished to step away from her.

'Come and meet some people.'

He took her hand and felt her tense as he led her across the ballroom.

'Relax,' he murmured, bending his head so that his mouth was against her ear and his breath stirred the tendrils of her hair. 'Tio Alvaro and his wife Lucia are nice. Just be yourself.'

Rafael introduced Juliet to his aunt and uncle and fielded their curiosity about where and when he had met his bride. He was conscious of the simmering look Juliet darted at him when he explained that it had been love at first sight when they had met in London.

Lucia glanced at Juliet's hand. 'I see you are not wearing an engagement ring. Shame on you, Rafael.'

'We married quickly—there wasn't time to choose a ring,' he said smoothly.

'Alvaro and I will be visiting London next month,' Lucia said to Juliet. 'I want to visit Buckingham Palace. Did you live near it?'

'Not very near,' she replied without a flicker.

Rafael pictured the tower block in the rough part of London where Juliet had lived, and was fiercely glad that she and her little daughter would never have to go back there.

'Where else do you recommend we visit while we're staying in the capital?' Lucia asked.

'Well, if you like music, or ballet, I recommend booking tickets for the Royal Albert Hall. It's a wonderful venue to enjoy a concert. Or there's the Royal Festival Hall and the Royal Opera House. All are spectacular.'

'I suppose you worked as a cleaner in the Opera House?' a voice said sarcastically.

Rafael looked round and saw Hector was standing close by. His grandfather had obviously been listening to the conversation. Furious with the old man, he tightened his arm around Juliet's waist, hoping she was not upset. *Dios*, his grandfather was a snob.

'Abuelo...' he began tensely.

'Actually, I danced at all three venues,' Juliet said calmly. 'I was a ballerina, and in my very brief career I performed on stage at several of London's best concert halls.'

Shock ran through Rafael. He heard Hector give a disbelieving snort but Tia Lucia clapped her hands together and said excitedly, 'I *love* the ballet—especially *Swan Lake*.'

'That's one of my favourites too,' Juliet said with a smile. 'I once performed the Dance of the Cygnets.'

'Do you still dance?' Lucia asked.

Juliet shook her head. 'Not professionally. I was badly injured in an accident and couldn't continue with my ballet career.'

Hector walked away and Rafael made an excuse, leaving Juliet to chat to his aunt and uncle, while he strode after his grandfather.

'Abuelo.' He caught up with the old man and scowled at him. It occurred to Rafael that he had spent all his adult life trying to win Hector's approval—without success. He *was* the best person to take over running the Casillas Group—he knew it and so did his grandfather. But he could never escape his gypsy heritage and the prejudice and mistrust it evoked—not just in his family but in people generally.

'Do not *ever* treat my wife with disrespect again,' he told Hector savagely. 'You have no right to make judgements upon her. You know nothing about Juliet.'

Hector's bushy brows rose. 'Do *you*?' he challenged.

He stared at Rafael, and the curiosity in his expression slowly changed into something which might have been begrudging respect. But maybe he'd imagined it, Rafael thought. And then he realised that he did not care about his grandfather's opinion of him. His only concern was that Hector would treat Juliet with the consideration and courtesy she deserved.

As he threaded his way back across the crowded ballroom he was waylaid by his half-brother. 'How are you, Francisco?' he greeted the young man.

'I'm in shock,' his brother said with a grin. 'Mamà has told me that you have a wife, but she seems to think it is suspicious that you married so quickly.'

Rafael knew it was not his half-brother's fault that their mother favoured him, her youngest son, and would do anything to see him succeed Hector. He did not like deceiving Frankie, but he could not risk Delfina discovering that his marriage was fake.

'No one was more surprised than me when I fell in love with Juliet,' he murmured. It was odd how easily the lie fell from his lips.

'I can't wait to meet the woman who finally persuaded you up the aisle. She must be amazing.'

'She certainly amazes *me*,' said Rafael, thinking of Juliet's latest startling revelation. 'I'll introduce you to her when I find her.'

He frowned as he scanned the ballroom but failed to see a sparkly gold dress.

Juliet stepped through the glass doors leading from the ballroom onto a wide balcony. Immediately the buzz of chattering voices and the music from the band became muted. It was a clear night, and she tipped her head back and studied the stars glittering like diamonds against the inky backdrop of the sky.

The party wasn't as daunting as she had expected, and apart from an awkward moment when Rafael's grandfather had made an unpleasant comment to her she was enjoying herself.

She had never dreamed when she'd been cleaning floors in the shopping centre that she would ever wear a beautiful ball gown, drink champagne and dance cheek to cheek—well, cheek to chest, she amended—with her impossibly handsome husband.

She leaned her elbows on the top of the stone balustrade and stared out over the dark garden. The mingled scents of jasmine and bougainvillea filled the air and she breathed deep, trying to slow the frantic thud of her pulse as she remembered the expression on Rafael's face when she had walked down the stairs in her glittering gold ball gown.

He had looked stunned—as if he couldn't believe it was her. And she understood the feeling because when she'd seen her reflection in the mirror after Sofia had applied the finishing touches to her make-up she had hardly recognised herself.

'My brother is in for a shock,' Sofia had said in a satisfied voice. 'You look amazing.'

Juliet *felt* amazing. Rafael had told her she looked beautiful and her heart had leapt when she'd seen the unmistakable gleam of desire in his green eyes. It had restored her pride after he'd looked at her with such disdain on the day of their wedding, when she had walked down the stairs at Ferndown House wearing that hideous dress.

But none of this was real, she reminded herself. Oh, the ball gown which shimmered every time she moved was real, as were the dozens of new outfits—some formal, some more casual, but all of them exorbitantly expensive—that filled her wardrobe. She had new shoes too: numerous pairs of elegant high heels made of softest Italian leather in a variety of colours, with matching handbags, and accessories including silk scarves and some pieces of modern, chunky costume jewellery made from semi-precious stones. She had thrown away all her old clothes, apart from a couple of leotards and her pointe shoes that she'd kept as reminders of her life as a ballerina.

Juliet knew it would easy to be swept away by the magic that had transformed her from looking and feeling unattractive to a realisation that she looked quite nice in clothes that fitted properly. But she must not forget the reason why Rafael had married her, and she must not allow herself to be seduced by a self-confessed playboy who had made clear his scathing opinion of love.

Not that she would be foolish enough to fall in love with him, she assured herself.

'Why are you out here alone?'

Rafael's gravelly voice sent a prickle of awareness across Juliet's skin and she spun round and found him standing close beside her. Much too close. Heat exploded inside her when his thigh brushed against hers.

He looked incredible, in a superbly tailored black tuxedo, white silk shirt and a black bow tie. A lock of his hair fell forward across his brow, and the shadow of black stubble covering his jaw gave him a rakish look that was spine-tinglingly sexy. Memories assailed her of the way he had held her tightly against his strong body while they had danced together. She had felt the warmth of his skin through his shirt and seen the shadow of his black chest hair beneath the fine silk. She'd wanted so badly to tear open the buttons and run her hands over his naked torso...

'I came outside for some air.' She gave him a

rueful smile. 'I am no more alone out here than in the ballroom, where I don't know anyone.'

'You know me.'

'Not really. We are strangers, thrown together in this crazy marriage.'

He frowned. 'We need to spend some time getting to know each other or we won't manage to convince my grandfather that our relationship is genuine. For a start, why didn't you mention before that you trained as a ballerina?'

'I didn't think you would be interested. You picked me to be your wife because you believed I was uncultured and came from a poor background.'

His jaw tightened. 'I have already apologised for the way I treated you.'

'You don't have to apologise when you're going to pay me five million pounds.'

If she kept reminding herself of the deal they had made she might find it easier to ignore the burning intensity in his gaze that made her wish their marriage was real in every sense.

Rafael exhaled heavily. 'The car accident that took your parents' lives also ended your dancing career, didn't it?'

'I had just danced the role of Giselle in London—one of the youngest ballerinas to have been chosen for the part.' Juliet hugged her arms around her. 'Mum and Dad died because of *me*,' she whispered. 'They were driving me to Birmingham, because the ballet was due to open next at the Symphony Hall there. I could have gone on the coach with the other dancers but my parents always came to my first night performances.'

'The accident was not your fault—you have to believe that,' Rafael said roughly. He pulled her into his arms and held her close to his chest. 'Thick fog and a speeding lorry—you had no control over those things.' He stroked his hand over her hair. 'It sounds as though your parents loved you very much.'

There was an odd note in his voice that Juliet could not define.

'They sacrificed so much so that I could follow my dream of being a ballerina,' she said. 'I won a scholarship to a boarding ballet school when I was eleven. The fees were paid but there were many other expenses, and my parents worked extra hours to buy my ballet shoes and cover all the costs.'

She sighed.

'I was the only scholarship student in my year and most of the other pupils were from wealthy families. I was made to feel that I didn't belong there by some of my peers because of my background. In the same way your grandfather made me feel that I was an outsider when you introduced me as your wife.'

Rafael's chest rose and fell. 'Why did you stay at the school if the other pupils upset you?'

'I was determined to be a ballerina and I didn't care about anything else. The other kids stopped teasing me when I consistently came top of the class in my dance exams. And I did make some friends. My best friend Chloe is the daughter of the famous art collector Derek Mullholland. I used to stay with her in the school holidays and her father would show us around his private art gallery and talk about the paintings.'

Beneath her ear Juliet heard the steady thud of Rafael's heart.

'Chloe is a soloist ballerina. We keep in touch, but I am envious of her career,' she admitted.

He said nothing, but he tightened his arms around her as if he understood, as if he cared—

*which of course he doesn't,* whispered her common sense.

'I plan to use some of your money to set up a dance school for children and young adults. My leg isn't strong enough for me to dance on the stage, but I can teach ballet and give other little girls the dream that I fulfilled for a short time.'

Juliet's heart missed a beat when she felt Rafael brush his lips over her hairline. Time seemed to be suspended and she did not know how long they stood there, with his arms wrapped around her and her cheek resting on his shirt front. But gradually she became aware of the hardness of his thighs pressing against her, and the heat of his body through his shirt.

The spicy scent of his cologne filled her senses, and when she looked up at him she discovered that he was staring at her with an intent expression that made her stomach swoop. She felt dizzy, as though she had drunk too much champagne, although she'd only had one glass.

He slid his hand beneath her chin and his eyes narrowed, gleaming with a sensual promise that set her pulse racing. Once again she had the feeling that none of this was real. It was a beautiful dream and she never wanted to wake up. Her eyelashes drifted closed and she felt Rafael's warm breath graze her lips.

'Open your eyes,' he commanded in a husky growl that sent a delicious shiver down her spine.

She obeyed, and as her gaze meshed with his she instinctively arched towards him as he angled his mouth over hers and kissed her. At first he kept it light, teasing her lips apart while he moved his hand from her jaw to cradle her cheek in his palm. He tasted divine and she pressed herself closer to him, wanting more, wanting…

'Oh!' Her soft gasp was muffled against his lips as he deepened the kiss, crushing her mouth beneath his so that her head was tilted back and she was powerless to resist his passionate onslaught.

Heat swept through her veins and a wildness bubbled up inside her as Rafael coaxed her lips apart in a kiss that transported her to a place where there was only sensation. He made a rough sound in his throat and moved his hand from her waist to the base of her spine, forcing her pelvis into contact with his so that she felt the powerful proof of his arousal.

Astounded that she could have such an effect on him, Juliet melted against him, lifting her arms to wind them around his neck while he pushed his tongue into her mouth and the kiss became ever more erotic.

Sparks shot through her. She hadn't known that a kiss could be like this: a conflagration that swept away her inhibitions and her uncertainty and compelled her to burn in Rafael's fire.

It took a few seconds for her to realise that the brilliant white lights she could see were not shooting stars but actual lights, which had been switched on to illuminate the balcony. Even more puzzling was the sound of applause.

Rafael lifted his mouth from hers and she turned her head to discover that they were in full view of the party guests in the ballroom—including his grandfather.

Understanding brought with it a wave of humiliation at the realisation that Rafael had kissed her so publicly in a bid to prove to Hector that their marriage was real. He must have known that the balcony lights were about to be turned on—or maybe he had instructed the staff to switch them on. Either way, that kiss had been under the spotlight…but only one of them had been acting.

Juliet wished a hole would appear beneath her feet and swallow her. But Rafael tightened his hold on her waist, as if he guessed that she wanted to tear herself out of his arms and slap his face. He strode across the balcony, giving her no choice but to walk with him back into the ballroom.

'I want to go and check on Poppy,' she muttered, making the excuse so that she could leave the party.

*She was such an idiot.* Rafael was a playboy, highly experienced in the art of seduction. And she had betrayed her fascination with him when she had responded to his heart-stopping kisses with an eagerness that made her cheeks burn when she remembered how she had come apart in his arms.

'You can't leave now. My grandfather is about to give his speech,' he told her. 'The nanny will see to Poppy if she wakes up.'

Hector stepped onto a dais at one end of the

room and looked around at the guests. 'As you all know, today I celebrate my eightieth birthday. The time has come for me to think about the future of the Casillas Group and consider who will be the best person to succeed me as Chairman and CEO. I believe that person is my eldest grandson Rafael.'

Juliet glanced around the room and was shocked by the look of fury on Delfina Casillas's haughty face. She wondered why Rafael's mother favoured her youngest son, and why there was no sign of affection between her and Rafael.

'However,' Hector continued, 'I have decided to remain as head of the company for the coming year, while I work closely with Rafael to ensure a smooth transition to his leadership. Rafael knows there are certain areas where he will need to prove his suitability before I step down. In my opinion, whoever ultimately succeeds me should be prepared to show commitment in all areas of his life—which is something that, frankly, Rafael has not done in the past. But his recent marriage suggests a change of heart.'

Hector paused, and from across the room

Juliet felt the old man's sharp black eyes flick from Rafael to her. She felt Rafael tighten his grip on her waist, pinning her to him.

'Perhaps,' Hector said thoughtfully, 'Rafael will be able to convince me to retire before the year is up.'

# CHAPTER SEVEN

'JULIET—WAIT.'

The sound of Rafael's voice behind her spurred Juliet on to increase her pace as she tore across the lawn, heading away from the twinkling lights of the mansion. But she wasn't used to walking, let alone running in high heels, with a long skirt swirling around her ankles, and he caught up with her in front of the chalet-style summerhouse.

His hand curled around her shoulder. 'Where are you going?'

'Anywhere as long as I'm far away from *you.*'

He swore and caught hold of her other shoulder, spinning her round to face him. 'What's the matter?'

The impatience in Rafael's voice fanned Juliet's temper. 'You are an expert at this game, but I'm just a novice and I don't know the rules,' she muttered.

Moonlight slid over his face, highlighting

his razor-edged cheekbones and hard jaw. The mouth that had lived up to its promise of heaven was set in a grim line and his brows were two black slashes on either side of his nose.

'What game? Why did you disappear from the ballroom while the guests were making a toast to my grandfather? People will think we have had a row.'

'I doubt it, after you made sure that everyone, including Hector, witnessed that X-rated snog on the balcony.' Juliet bit her lip. She felt such a fool. 'I opened up to you in a way that I have never done with anyone else,' she told him rawly. 'I thought you'd kissed me because— Oh, not because you *cared*, but I thought you liked me a little. I should have realised it was an ideal opportunity for you to act the role of a loving husband in front of your grandfather when you found me on the balcony. The stage was set and all you needed were lights and action.'

To her horror, her voice wobbled, and she cringed because she could not disguise her hurt feelings. Just because she was wearing a beautiful dress it did not change who she was.

She was still a single mother from a council estate, and no amount of clever tailoring could give the illusion that she had the kind of curvaceous figure that Rafael preferred—if the newspaper pictures of his last busty blonde mistress were anything to go by.

She shrugged her shoulders, trying to throw off his hands, but he held her tighter. A muscle flickered in his cheek when she dashed a hand across her wet eyes.

'That was not why I kissed you,' he said harshly. 'It had nothing to do with my grandfather. I didn't know that those damn lights would come on.'

'You can't deny it was convenient that we were lit up like a Christmas tree. And Hector hinted in his speech that he might make you CEO in less than a year, so I can't complain. The sooner he hands you the company the sooner we can end our farce of a marriage.'

'I did not know that we would be seen by everyone in the ballroom.'

Rafael's voice was as dangerous as the rigid set of his jaw. He trapped her gaze, and her breath hitched in her throat when she saw heat and hunger flash in his eyes.

'I kissed you because I couldn't resist you,' he said tensely. 'Because I'd wanted to kiss you since I watched you float down the stairs looking like a princess in that golden dress with your hair like amber silk. Looking like every red-blooded male's fantasy woman.'

She shook her head, not allowing herself to believe him. 'What man would fantasise about *me*?' she whispered.

'This man, *chiquita*,' he growled.

He jerked her towards him, taking her by surprise, so that she slammed hard into his chest and the air was forced out of her lungs. Before she could draw a breath he'd lowered his head and claimed her mouth in a kiss of blatant possession and savage passion.

Her brain told her to resist him. Insisted she would be a fool to believe him. But there had been something so stark in his voice. And she *wanted* this, Juliet admitted to herself. She wanted his mouth on hers, kissing her with an urgency that was too fierce to be fake.

The world spun on its axis as he swept her into his arms and carried her along the path to the summerhouse, shouldered open the door and kicked it shut behind him while his lips remained fused to hers.

Moonlight shone through the windows and filled the summerhouse with a pearly gleam. Rafael strode over to the sofa that took up one corner of the room and sat down, settling her on his lap. He traced his lips over her cheek, nuzzled the tender place behind her ear and then nipped her earlobe with his sharp teeth, sending starbursts of pleasure through her entire body.

And then his mouth was on hers once more and he was kissing her—unhurriedly at first, and then with increasing passion when she responded to him with a fervency that made him groan. His pressed his lips to the pulse beating erratically at the base of her throat before he kissed his way along her collarbone.

Juliet felt his hand on the bare skin of her back and only realised that he had tugged the zip of her dress down when the strapless bodice fell away from her breasts. The air felt cool on her heated skin and her nipples swelled and hardened beneath Rafael's avid gaze.

'No bra,' he said thickly.

'I'm too small to need one.' Her tiny breasts were a constant regret to her.

'You're perfect.'

Dark colour ran along his cheekbones when he cupped one breast in his hand. Reaction shivered through Juliet as he rubbed his thumb-pad across her nipple, teasing the sensitive peak so that she made a choked sound. The pleasure of his touch was so intense that she could not control the little quivers that ran through her. Rafael was a sorcerer and she was spellbound by his magic.

She held her breath when he lowered his head to her breast. Moonbeams danced across his dark hair and Juliet sank her fingers into the rich silk as he captured her nipple between his lips and flicked his tongue back and forth over the dusky tip.

Darts of pleasure shot down to the molten place between her legs. Her ability to think was lost in the wondrous sensations he was creating with his mouth and his hands on her body. She was startled to realise that the husky moans that bounced off the walls of the summerhouse were coming from her throat.

Rafael pulled the bodice of her dress down

so that it bunched at her waist and then leaned his head against the back of the sofa, his eyes glittering as he subjected her to a slow appraisal.

'You are exquisite,' he said, in a rough tone that made Juliet ache everywhere.

He cradled the pale mounds of her breasts in his big hands and played with her reddened nipples. The ache deep in her pelvis became an insistent throb. When he shifted their position, so that she was lying on the sofa and he was stretched out on top of her, she gloried in his weight pressing her into the cushions. He nudged her legs apart with his thigh and she felt the hard length of his arousal press against her feminine core through the dress.

And all the while Rafael kissed her with a mastery that made her shake with an incandescent need that blazed and burned until she was only aware of the heat of his body and the sweep of his hands across her skin.

He lifted the hem of her dress and skimmed a path up to her thighs, tracing his fingers over her tiny lace panties. Lost in the sheer delight of his caresses, Juliet held her breath and willed him to move his fingers higher. She shuddered when he dipped into the waistband of her knickers and stroked his finger lightly over her moist opening.

It was a very long time since a man had touched her so intimately. There had only been one other man before Rafael and she didn't want to think about Bryan and her solitary, uninspiring experience of sex with him. But the word floated in her mind. Was that where this was leading? Did Rafael want to have sex with her?

He was as hard as a spike beneath his trousers, and she imagined him pulling his zip down and pushing the panel of her panties aside so that he could drive his erection into her.

She was eager for him to make love to her. But like this? A frantic coupling in the dark in a glorified shed before they returned to his grandfather's birthday party?

More importantly, she wasn't prepared for sex—and while she had forgiven herself for one accidental pregnancy, two would be utterly irresponsible.

Even so, the temptation she felt to allow Rafael to continue caressing her with his clever fingers was strong, and her body throbbed with unfulfilled longing when she tore her mouth from his.

*'I'm not on the pill.'*

Rafael froze as Juliet's words kick-started his brain, which until that moment had been clouded in a red haze of desire. His first reaction was frustration that he wasn't carrying condoms in his jacket, as he invariably did on evenings out in London. He saw nothing wrong with one-night stands if both parties understood the rules.

But Juliet was not a woman he had picked up in a nightclub—she was his wife. In name only. That was what he had assured her when he'd suggested their marriage deal, and in all honesty he hadn't expected that he would *want* to take his unappealing bride who had behaved like a sullen teenager at the register office to bed.

He had been blind to her beauty and unaware of her vulnerability, which was evident now in her wary expression as he lifted himself off her and offered her his hand to pull her up from the sofa. The shadowy interior of the summerhouse could not disguise the flush that spread over her cheeks as she dragged the top of her dress up to cover her breasts.

'Will you zip me up?'

She presented her back to him and his stomach clenched as he pushed her silky fall of hair over one fragile shoulder so that he could fasten her dress.

'I can't face going back to the ballroom,' she said in low voice.

Rafael studied her kiss-stung lips and the betraying hard points of her nipples, visible through her dress, and it occurred to him that his grandfather would have no doubt that his marriage was real if he saw evidence that he and Juliet had slipped away from the party to indulge their passion for each other.

But he couldn't bring himself to humiliate her in front of his family, who had already judged her so harshly because of their misplaced belief that money and an aristocratic lineage made them better than a cash-strapped single mother.

He looked away from her, struggling to bring his rampant libido under control. 'You can go into the house via the kitchens and use the back staircase to go up to the apartment so that no one sees you. I'll say that you were feeling unwell and have gone to bed.'

'Thank you.'

Instead of walking out of the summerhouse when he opened the door she stood on her tiptoes and pressed her lips to his cheek. His pulse kicked when he breathed in her feminine fragrance—perfume mixed with something muskier that clung to his fingers—and he recognised the scent of her womanhood.

'Rafael…'

He did not want a post mortem on what had happened between them. What definitely should not have happened and what must not happen again.

'I should get back to the party before my absence is noticed,' he said.

The flash of hurt in her eyes at his abrupt tone convinced him that he should have listened to the warning voice in his head when she'd fled from the party and he had chased after her.

Rafael stayed in the ballroom until after midnight, when the last of the guests departed.

His grandfather had retired to bed some time ago and it had given him an excuse to remain downstairs and act as host.

When he entered his private suite he headed straight for his study and spent another half an hour there, nursing a large cognac. Juliet would surely be asleep by now, he thought as he entered his dressing room and threw a pile of bedding onto the sofa.

His cufflinks hit the dressing table, followed by his tie. He shrugged out of his shirt and undid his trousers, wincing when the zip brushed against his manhood, which was still semi-aroused several hours after he'd nearly lost his sanity in the summerhouse.

'I only discovered today that this is where you have been sleeping.'

Juliet's soft voice came from the doorway between the master bedroom and the dressing room.

'I assumed there were two bedrooms in the apartment and you were using the second one.'

He glanced at her and felt his blood rush south, his erection instantly and embarrassingly hard. Juliet had shimmered in the sequined ball gown, but in a black satin chemise with semi-transparent lace bra cups that exposed a tantalising amount of her small but perfectly formed breasts she simmered with sensual promise.

Once again he wondered how he could have dismissed her as drab. The uncomfortable truth was that he had seen what he'd wanted to see, Rafael acknowledged. The irony of finding himself fiercely attracted to his little sexpot wife wasn't lost on him.

'There is only a master bedroom in my private suite. Obviously the house has other bedrooms—twenty-five, I believe, although I have never counted them. But we need Hector to think we are sleeping together.'

'I can't imagine that sofa is comfortable for someone of your height...' Juliet hesitated and a rosy stain ran under her skin. 'We could share the bed. I mean—it's huge. Big enough for us to keep to our own sides of the mattress... unless you want...'

Her voice trailed off and the shy look she gave him very nearly made him forget that she was off limits.

'No,' he said curtly. 'That would be a bad idea.'

The pink flush on her cheeks spilled down her throat and across the upper slopes of her breasts, tempting him to rip the confection of satin and lace from her body, sweep her into his arms and carry her through to the bedroom so that they could both enjoy that big, soft bed—but not to sleep in.

He knew it was what Juliet wanted him to do. Her pupils were dilated so that her eyes were dark discs rimmed with brilliant blue. But he suspected that she wanted her sexual gratification wrapped up in a romantic ideal that he was incapable of giving her.

'I didn't get the impression earlier tonight that you thought our sharing a bed was a bad idea.' Her tongue darted out across her bottom lip. 'In the summerhouse—'

'What happened between us there was a mistake.'

'You wanted to make love…and so did I.'

*Dios*, why not take what she was offering and satisfy his libido? Rafael asked himself. If Juliet expected hearts and flowers that was *her* problem.

But the nagging voice of his conscience insisted that he was responsible for her. She had no idea what he was. He had been born in the gutter and had grown up in a slum where every day had been a fight to survive. He knew how to keep himself together, but that was all he knew. There was nothing inside him but darkness and ruthless ambition.

Juliet had lost her parents when she had still been a teenager and he sensed her loneliness. She was looking for love, affection, caring— but he could not give her those things. How could he when he had never experienced them?

'I wanted sex,' he told her bluntly. 'To scratch an itch. And you happened to be there.'

The colour drained from her face as quickly as it had appeared. 'So you're saying that any woman would have done?'

Her eyelashes swept down, but not before he'd seen a wounded expression that gutted him.

Juliet was silent for a moment before her chin came up. Rafael though of all the other times she had picked herself up after life had delivered another knockout blow. Admiration curled through him when she met his gaze steadily. Only the faint tremor of her bottom lip betrayed her hurt, but she quickly firmed her mouth.

'Then there is nothing more to be said. But it's ridiculous for you to sleep on the sofa when I am so much smaller than you and will fit on it much better. You can have the bed and I'll sleep here.'

She turned towards the sofa and started to make up a bed. When she bent over to smooth out the sheet her satin chemise pulled tight across her pert derrière. Rafael swore beneath his breath. She would tempt a saint, let alone the sinner he knew himself to be.

He snatched a pillow out of her hands. 'Leave it,' he said savagely. 'Go—now—before I do something that we will both regret.'

Juliet's eyes widened. But she must have realised that his self-control was at breaking point and without another word she sped back into the bedroom and slammed the door behind her.


Juliet put off taking Poppy down to breakfast for as long as possible. She knew that Rafael was in the habit of drinking several cups of black coffee in the morning, while he sat on

the balcony and glanced at the day's newspapers before he left for work at the Casillas
Group's offices in Valencia. But she couldn't
face seeing him.

She was mortified at the memory of how she
had thrown herself at him and he had rejected
her, so she read Poppy two more stories until
the little girl hopped off the bed and ran over
to the door.

'I'm hungry, Mummy.'

It was past nine o'clock—he must have left
by now. 'Okay, munchkin. I'm coming.'

She followed her daughter into the kitchen
and her heart leapt into her mouth when she
saw that the bi-fold doors were open and Rafael was outside, sitting at the table with a
newspaper propped against the coffee jug.

Poppy greeted him excitedly and climbed
onto the chair beside him. 'Raf, will you read
me *The Three Bears*?'

'Rafael has to go to work,' Juliet said quickly.
She avoided his gaze and fussed over Poppy's
breakfast. 'Would you like a peach with your
yoghurt?'

'I'm not going to work today,' he told Poppy.
'And I'll read the book if you eat all your break-

fast.' He picked up the cafetière and looked at Juliet. 'Coffee?'

'Thank you,' she said stiffly, feeling her colour rise.

Her unsubtle suggestion that they should share the bed came back to mock her. She wished she didn't blush so easily. She wished Rafael wasn't wearing sunglasses which hid his expression. She wished she could prevent her eyes from straying to his broad chest and the denim shirt that was open at the neck, revealing a sprinkling of black chest hair.

Thankful that her body's reaction to his sexual magnetism was hidden beneath her robe, she hugged her coffee cup like a security blanket while Poppy chatted away to Rafael. His patience with the little girl surprised Juliet again, and made her wonder why he had been so vehement when he'd said he did not want children of his own.

She looked up when the nanny stepped onto the balcony. 'Would Poppy like to come and play with the twins in the garden?'

'Keep your sun hat on,' Juliet instructed as Poppy trotted off with Elvira.

She really did not want to be alone with Rafael, but just as she was about to rise from the table he pushed a plate of *churros*—little sticks of dough which had been deep-fried and sprinkled with sugar and cinnamon—towards her.

'You should have some breakfast.'

'I'm not hungry,' she muttered, her chair scraping on the stone floor as she stood up.

'Sit down and eat.'

Rafael's exasperated tone made Juliet feel like a naughty child. After a moment's hesitation she sank back down onto her chair.

'Sulking is not an attractive trait,' he drawled.

'I am *not* sulking.' Releasing her breath slowly helped to control her temper. 'I'm tired of the games you play. You blow hot and cold. I don't know where I am with you, or what you want from me, and frankly I don't care.'

She forced herself to look directly at him and ignored the leap of her pulse. Okay, he was so gorgeous that her heart did a flip every time she looked at him. *Get over it,* she told herself. He was also unbelievably arrogant and had an ego the size of a planet.

To her surprise, Rafael looked away first. 'We are having lunch with my mother and her husband Alberto. My dear *mamà* is desperate for my grandfather to choose my half-brother as his successor and she will do anything to discredit me.' His voice was emotionless. 'Delfina must not suspect that our marriage is fake.'

'I'll do my best to pretend that I think you're God's gift to womankind,' Juliet told him flippantly.

His heavy brows lowered. 'Do not test my patience, *chiquita*.'

'Or you'll do what?'

He pulled off his sunglasses and scowled at her. But the hard gleam in his eyes was not temper but desire, and the heat of it scorched Juliet even as it confused her.

Last night he had told her that he'd wanted sex with any woman who was conveniently to hand and it had happened to be her. But he was staring at her now as if she really was his fantasy woman—as if she was the only woman he wanted.

The air was so still that she could hear the rasp of his breath and the unevenness of hers. Awareness prickled across her skin. Sexual tension sizzled between them and suddenly she was afraid—not of Rafael, but of the way he made her feel. The way she made *him* feel if the hunger in his gaze was real…

She broke eye contact and took a deep breath. 'You said we should get to know each other so that we can convince Hector and other members of your family that we are genuinely a couple. I've told you a lot about me, but I know virtually nothing about you.'

He put his shades on again and leaned back in his chair, watching her. She had no idea what he was thinking.

'What do you want to know?'

'Why is there such animosity between you and your mother?'

He shrugged. 'A clash of personalities.'

'I assume your parents are divorced as your mother is remarried and you have a half-brother? Do you keep in contact with your father?'

'No.'

The word shot from him like a bullet.

Juliet said nothing, and he must have realised that she was waiting for him to continue because after a moment he muttered, 'My father died years ago.'

'I'm sorry.'

'Don't be,' he said harshly. 'I'm not.'

She could not hide her shock. 'That's a terrible thing to say about your own father.'

'He was a terrible man.'

Rafael shoved a hand through his hair, and although Juliet could not see the expression in his eyes she sensed that he was agitated—something she would not have believed possible for a man whose self-control was formidable.

'I suppose you will find out about my background at some point, so it might as well be now,' he muttered.

Juliet suddenly remembered that his sister had said something about how she and Rafael had felt overawed when they had come to live at the Casillas mansion.

'My mother eloped with my father because my grandfather disapproved of her relationship with him. Ivan Mendoza had a gardening job on the Casillas estate and apparently Delfina fell madly in love with him.' Rafael grimaced. 'I remember he could be charming to people when it suited him, but he was never anything other than violent and aggressive to me.'

She froze. 'Did your father hit you?'

'Frequently—until I learned to dodge his fists and run away when he undid his belt.'

'How old were you when he started hitting you?'

He shrugged. 'I don't remember a time when I wasn't afraid of him.'

Juliet felt sick, imagining Rafael as a little boy, perhaps no older than Poppy, being physically abused by his father. 'What about your mother? Didn't she try to protect you?'

'I don't know if my mother was aware when she married Ivan that he was involved in the drug scene. He was a petty crook, who worked when he could find a job, and had a sideline in drug dealing.' Rafael exhaled heavily. 'I think it's likely that my mother was a drug user then—probably encouraged into that lifestyle by Ivan. I have very few memories of her before she left. She was distant, uninterested—especially in me. I don't remember her ever showing me affection.'

'What do you mean when you say that your mother left?'

'She disappeared out of my life when I was about seven. Sofia would have been around two years old. I didn't find out my actual birth date until years later, when I saw my birth certificate,' he explained. 'My father never said where my mother had gone.' A nerve flickered in his cheek. 'I think my sister missed our mother at first and she clung to me.'

Juliet thought of her happy childhood, with parents who had adored her, and her heart ached for Rafael and his sister. 'Who took care of you and Sofia?'

He gave another shrug. 'My father was a *gitano*—a gypsy. The Roma community is tightknit, and *gitanos* have a strong sense of family. Sometimes the other mothers took care of Sofia and gave us food. But my father was always moving around and we didn't settle anywhere for long—which is why it was years before my grandfather found us.'

He caught Juliet's questioning look.

'My mother had returned to the Casillas mansion. Presumably she missed the wealth and status of belonging to one of Spain's foremost families,' he said drily. 'I don't know why she did not take us or at least my sister with her when she left. We ended up living with my father in a slum outside Madrid, where drugs were dealt openly on the streets and criminal gangs were in charge. We were there for a few years before Ivan was shot dead in a gang war and Sofia and I were placed in an orphanage. Once there was an official record of our whereabouts Hector managed to track us down, and he brought us to live at the Casillas mansion when I was twelve.'

Juliet was so shocked by Rafael's description of his childhood that she did not know what to say. It explained the toughness she sensed in him, and his obsessive determination to get what he wanted.

'Your mother must have been happy to be reunited with you and your sister...' she murmured.

He gave a short laugh. 'I was a surly teenager, with a chip on my shoulder and a hot temper. *None* of my relatives—including my mother—were pleased to have me around, although I'm glad to say that Sofia was made more welcome.' He gave a faint smile. 'My sister learned young how to smile and say the right things to people. I was far less amenable. But my grandfather saw something in me and pushed me to catch up on my education. Meanwhile my mother had married a distant cousin, and my half-brother Francisco is a *true* Casillas, in Delfina's opinion, and should be Hector's successor.'

Rafael picked up his coffee cup and swallowed its contents.

'You said you were made to feel that you did not belong at your ballet school by some of the richer pupils. I understand what it's like to feel like an outsider, because that's how I felt when I came to live here with my aristocratic family. Many of my relatives still think that a *gitano* is not good enough to be a Casillas.'

Juliet stared at him. 'Yet even knowing that your family would despise me, you brought me here and presented me as your wife. You didn't consider my feelings. Perhaps,' she said huskily, 'you thought I was too unintelligent to *have* feelings.'

His jaw clenched. 'I have never thought you unintelligent. I admit that when I first met you it crossed my mind that it would infuriate Hector if my bride was a single mother from a council estate...'

Juliet blanched and he swore.

'You have shown me that I was wrong to make assumptions about you based on the circumstances I found you in. But I won't lie to you. I needed to marry quickly, and your financial problems gave me the leverage to persuade you to be my wife.'

Rafael's voice was indecipherable, and his eyes were still hidden behind his sunglasses so that Juliet had no clue to his thoughts.

'Was my decision cold and calculating? Yes.' He answered his own question before she could speak. 'I told you once that my pursuit of power is a ruthless game, with no place for weakness or emotions—and nothing has changed.'

# CHAPTER EIGHT

SOMETHING *HAD* CHANGED. Rafael suspected it was something inside him, but he refused to examine that unsettling thought and assured himself that the change was entirely in Juliet.

It was not only her appearance, he brooded, studying her where she sat opposite him at the dining table in his mother's over-fussy suite. The truth was that he hadn't been able to take his eyes off his wife throughout this tedious lunch with Delfina and her tedious husband.

Juliet looked deliciously cool and elegant in a pale blue silk sheath dress that skimmed her slender figure. The neckline was decorous, but cut just low enough to reveal the upper slopes of her breasts. Those perfect small handfuls that made Rafael's mouth water when he pictured the dusky pink nipples he had tasted once. He had come to the conclusion that he would *have* to lick and suckle them again—

if his overheated body did not spontaneously combust first.

He forced his mind away from the erotic images and shifted in his seat in a bid to ease the uncomfortable tightness of his trousers stretched across his arousal. *Dios*, no other woman had ever made his heart pound the way Juliet did, nor made him feel like a hormone-fuelled youth instead of a self-confessed cynic who had become jaded with easy sex.

He was used to having whichever woman he wanted with minimum effort from him, but he had discovered that there was such a thing as too much choice, Rafael acknowledged sardonically.

Juliet's daughter was sitting beside her. Despite Poppy's young age she had behaved impeccably during lunch. She was a cute kid, he conceded. But like her mother Poppy had a way of looking directly into his eyes that disconcerted him. As if she saw something inside him that Rafael was quite certain did not exist.

'I did not expect that you would bring the child with you,' Delfina had said when he'd carried the little girl into the private apartment. Beside him, Juliet had stiffened as his mother had added coldly, 'Couldn't you have left her with the nanny?'

'Elvira offered to look after Poppy, but I like to spend as much time as possible with my daughter,' Juliet had replied calmly, but Rafael had caught the gleam of battle in her blue eyes.

Now Alberto was chatting to Juliet about three of Pablo Picasso's paintings, which he owned. Rafael knew his mother did not share her husband's interest in the famous Spanish painter, and she'd looked irritated when Juliet had revealed an impressive knowledge of the artist's work.

'Did your parents have professions?' Delfina asked during a lull in conversation.

'They both worked at a hospital.'

'Oh! Were they doctors?'

'Dad was a porter and Mum was a domestic assistant,' Juliet said cheerfully.

Delfina's brows arched in a supercilious expression. 'Domestic work seems to be a favourite in your family.'

'Madre…' Rafael said warningly. His mother could be a bitch and he would *not* allow her to upset Juliet.

'My parents worked hard so that I could follow my dream of becoming a ballerina. They were not rich, or particularly well educated, but they loved me and supported me.' Juliet looked directly at Delfina. 'They would never have abandoned me in a crime-ridden slum as you did Rafael and his sister when they were young children—Sofia just a baby and Rafael only seven years old.'

Delfina drew a sharp breath, but Juliet was continuing in a fierce voice.

'How *could* you have left your children with a father who was cruel and violent? You must have known that Ivan beat Rafael with his belt—'

Her voice cracked and a chink opened up in Rafael's heart.

His mother had paled and her highly glossed lips were a scarlet slash across her face. 'How dare you...?' Delfina breathed.

'I dare because I am Rafael's wife. And it is a wife's duty to stand by her husband. I was appalled when Rafael told me about how he suffered as a child, living in a slum.'

Juliet brushed her hand across her eyes and Rafael felt a jolt of something he could not explain when he saw that her lashes were wet.

'Hector brought him to the Casillas mansion to be reunited with you and his other relatives but he was made to feel unwelcome and unwanted. *You* did not defend him, but I will. Rafael is Hector's eldest grandson and *he* should succeed his grandfather as head of the Casillas Group.'

In the stunned silence that followed Rafael told himself that the pain he felt beneath his breastbone was indigestion...too much rich food. The ache could not be because Juliet had stood up for him, *fought* for him in a way that no one had ever done in his entire life. As if he mattered. To *her.*

His mother picked up her wine glass and drained it before she looked at Rafael. 'I was ashamed,' she said tightly.

'I know, Madre. You have always made it clear that you are ashamed of having a son who is part-*gitano*. I will never be the perfect son, like Francisco, but the CEO-ship *is* my birthright and I *will* claim my place within the family and the company.'

Delfina did not speak again, although as Rafael bade her goodbye and kissed the air close to her cheek he had an odd sense that she wanted to say something to him.

'Are you angry with me?' Juliet muttered as they walked through the house back to his apartment.

He glanced at her over Poppy's head. The little girl was walking between them and had insisted on holding his hand as well as Juliet's.

'Why would I be angry? You acted the role of supportive wife very convincingly.'

He opened the door of his apartment and as Juliet preceded him inside her long hair brushed against his arm and he breathed in the lemony scent of the shampoo she used.

Poppy spied her favourite teddy bear and ran across the room.

Juliet turned to him. 'I wasn't acting. What happened to you when you were a child was terrible. Your mother shouldn't have deserted you, and her failure to protect you has had a fundamental effect on you. I think it could be the reason why you have never allowed yourself to fall in love. You're afraid of being let down and abandoned, like Delfina abandoned you before.'

Her words opened that chink in his heart a

little wider, and Rafael didn't know what to make of that—or her.

'I think you should stop trying to psycho-analyse me,' he said drily. 'And you should certainly stop looking for my redeeming features, because I don't have any.'

She shook her head. 'You took care of your sister—acted as a parent to her when you were just a child yourself. When I met you I thought you had only ever known wealth and privilege. The fact that you spent the first twelve years of your life in a slum doesn't make you less of a man, it makes you *more* of one—a better person than any of your pampered relatives who have no right to look down on you.'

'A better man would not have sat through lunch imagining stripping you naked and having wild sex with you on my mother's dining table,' he rasped.

Rosy colour winged along her high cheek-bones, but she held his gaze. 'That itch still bothering you, is it?'

'You have no idea, *chiquita...*' He could not explain the restlessness inside him that seemed to get a whole lot worse when she smiled. 'I need to disabuse you of the idea that there is anything good in me.'

Juliet tilted her head to one side and looked at him thoughtfully. 'I wonder why you are so determined to do that,' she said softly.

Before he could reply—and the truth was that he did not *how* to respond—she walked away from him in the direction of her dressing room.

'Sofia has asked me to give Ana and Inez some ballet lessons. We're going to have our first dancing class this afternoon—unless there's anything else you want me to do?'

A number of highly erotic scenarios flooded his mind, which had an immediate and predictable effect on his body.

'I promised to play golf with Tio Alvaro,' he growled, his feet already taking him towards the door of the apartment and safety—away from the temptation of his wife who was not his wife. Not in any way that mattered. And Rafael was beginning to think that it mattered a lot.

Three hours spent on the Casillas estate's private golf course would ordinarily have given him time to clear his head.

'You seem to be distracted,' his uncle commented as they walked off the green. Alvaro was jubilant because he had won the game convincingly. 'I suppose you are thinking about business?'

Rafael hadn't spared a single thought for any of the business projects which until recently he had been obsessed with. The realisation that his new obsession with Juliet was interfering not just with his game of golf but with his focus on the company was disturbing. Work had always been his number one priority—the only mistress to command his fidelity.

The situation could not continue, he brooded. Juliet had got under his skin and there was only one way to deal with his unexpected fascination with her.

There was no one around when he entered the mansion. Most of his relatives and the household staff took a siesta in the afternoons, but as he walked across the entrance hall he heard music coming from the ballroom. Puzzled, he opened the door—and stopped dead when he saw Juliet dancing.

Rafael knew nothing about ballet, but he could tell instinctively that she was a talented ballerina. Dressed in a black leotard that revealed her ultra-slender figure, she seemed to glide across the floor on the points of her ballet shoes. Ethereal and graceful, strong and yet fragile. She did not simply dance to the music she lived it, breathed it, painting pictures in the air with each twirl and leap as if she had wings and could fly.

He stepped into the room and quietly closed the door, leaning against it while he watched her. He was utterly captivated...mesmerised. As a boy growing up in the slums he'd had no idea that such beauty existed. He could not take his eyes off her supple body, and his breath became trapped in his lungs as desire swept molten and hot through his veins, setting him ablaze everywhere.

Juliet danced with such passion, such fire, and he wanted all of it.

But her performance ended abruptly when she leapt into the air and seemed to land awkwardly. She gave a cry as she crumpled to the floor, trembling like a bird with a broken wing...a bird that could no longer soar into the sky.

Rafael's heart gave a jolt when he heard the sound of her weeping.

'*Dios, querida*, are you badly hurt?'

He was across the ballroom in seconds and kneeling on the floor beside her. 'Juliet, *cariño*,' he said huskily as she lifted her face and he saw tears streaming down her cheeks.

'My stupid leg.'

The words hung there, hurting him as much as she was hurting. Her voice ached with a depth of emotion he could barely comprehend. Loss—of her parents, and her ballet career, and more than that. The loss of the unique gift that Rafael had glimpsed when he'd watched her dance.

He had no idea what to say to her. 'You must miss dancing.'

'Ballet was my life,' she said, in a low voice that scraped his insides. 'It was like breathing—a necessary part of me. But now it's gone.'

'But you can still dance. You are incredible, *querida*.'

She scrubbed a hand over her eyes. 'I can manage for a few minutes, but I'll never be able to dance professionally. My leg isn't strong enough to cope with the relentless routine of rehearsals and performances, the pursuit of perfection. There's a reason why the life of a ballet dancer is called a beautiful agony.'

Her wry smile floored Rafael. The lack of self-pity in her voice humbled him, and that chink in his heart opened wider still.

'Come,' he said softly, lifting her into his arms.

'I can walk,' she protested as he carried her across the ballroom. 'I'll have a bath. It helps to relax the muscles in my thigh.'

'Put your arms around my neck,' he commanded, liking the feel of her small breasts pressed against his chest when she complied.

He strode up the stairs, and when he entered his apartment headed straight into the en suite bathroom and placed her on a chair. He ran a bath, tipping a liberal amount of scented bath crystals into the water.

He turned to find her watching him, and the lost look in her blue eyes, the shimmer of tears, evoked a reaction inside him that was too complicated for him to deal with right then.

Instead he knelt in front of her and curled his

fingers around the edge of her leotard. 'Let's get you undressed and into the bath.'

'I can manage. Please…' she whispered when he didn't move. 'I want to be alone. I don't need your help.'

Her rejection was no more than he deserved, Rafael acknowledged. But it hurt more than it should—more than he would have believed possible when he had prided himself for nigh on thirty years in not allowing anyone the power to hurt him.

He stood up and stared at her downbent head. Her hair was arranged in a classical bun that showed off the delicate line of her jaw and her slender neck.

'Don't lock the door,' he said tautly. 'I don't want to have to break it down if you have a problem.'

Juliet lay back in the roll-top bath and felt the ache in her thigh start to ease in the warm water. She had been an idiot to dance on points, she thought ruefully. But giving a dancing lesson to Rafael's nieces had reminded her of how she had fallen in love with ballet when she had learned those first simple steps as a child.

After the class Sofia had taken the twins and Poppy to play in the garden, and Juliet had found the temptation to dance in the huge ballroom too strong to resist.

She closed her eyes and allowed her mind to run over the other events of the day. Rafael's shocking revelations about his childhood, when his mother had abandoned him to his fate with his violent father. It had made her want to cry when he'd told her his story, and she hadn't been able to control her anger when they'd had lunch with his mother.

She did not care about Delfina's haughty disdain of her, but Rafael deserved better than to be treated like an outsider by the Casillas family.

The water was cooling and she rested her arms on the edge of the bath while she levered herself upright. Her thigh muscle spasmed and she couldn't hold back a yelp of pain.

Immediately the bathroom door flew open and Rafael appeared, glowering at her. 'What happened? Your leg...?'

'It's fine. It just twinged a bit.'

She caught her bottom lip between her teeth when it belatedly occurred to her that she was naked, standing there in the bath with water streaming down her body. Rafael was staring at her with an intensity that caused her stomach to swoop, and now his gaze dropped down from her breasts to the neatly trimmed triangle of pale red curls between her legs.

Her skin, already pink from being immersed in hot water, flushed even pinker, and there was nothing she could do to prevent her nipples from hardening so that they jutted provocatively, as if begging for his attention.

'Go away…' she muttered.

'You've got to be kidding.'

His rough voice rasped over her, setting each nerve-ending alight. The fierce glitter in his eyes caused her heart to kick in her chest as he walked purposefully across the bathroom.

She licked her dry lips and saw his eyes narrow on the movement of her tongue. 'Will you pass me a towel?'

He took a towel from the shelf and held it out to her. But when she unfolded it, she discovered that it wasn't a big bath sheet but a hand towel that was too small to cover her nakedness. *Seriously?*

His mouth curved into a wicked grin that

destroyed her flimsy defences like skittles tumbling after a strike. Modesty dictated that she should at least hold her hands in front of the pertinent areas of her body, to hide them from his hot gaze. But instead she burned in the fire that danced golden and bright in his green eyes.

'Rafael...' she whispered, with so much longing in her breathy voice that he gave a chuckle as he settled his hands on either side of her waist and lifted her out of the bath. 'I'll make you wet.'

She caught her breath when he settled her against him, so that one of his arms was around her back and the other beneath her knees, and carried her through to the bedroom.

'Not as wet as I am about to make you, *chiquita.*'

The promise in his voice echoed the desire in his eyes. His skin was stretched taut over the blades of his cheekbones, giving him a feral look that sent a quiver through Juliet. She felt boneless, and when he bent his head and angled his mouth over hers she parted her lips and gave herself up to the sweet seduction of his kiss.

The room tilted as he lowered her onto the bed and leaned over her, running his hands over her body from her hips up to her breasts, scalding her skin wherever he touched. She wanted him to surrender to the passion that she sensed he was controlling with his formidable willpower. What would it be like to see that control shatter? Would she survive the tsunami?

'You said that any woman would do,' she reminded him.

'I lied.'

His husky admission dispatched her doubts. He stopped nuzzling her neck and claimed her mouth once more, gentle seduction replaced by hungry demands that she was powerless to deny. He had fascinated her from the start, and she shuddered with delight when he moved down her body and flicked his tongue across one pebble-hard nipple and then the other, again and again, until the pleasure was too intense and she gave a keening cry.

Eyes closed, she felt the scrape of his beard over her belly—her thighs. Her eyelashes flew open. 'What are you doing?'

He lifted his head, amusement and something else that made her stomach muscles contract glinting in his narrowed gaze. 'What do you *think* I am about to do, *chiquita*?'

'I have no idea.'

His low laugh rolled through her and she tried to twitch her thighs together, to hide the betraying dampness of her arousal that scented the air.

'You cannot really be so innocent,' Rafael said half beneath his breath as he pulled her hips towards him, so that her bottom was on the edge of the bed, and dropped to the floor on his knees.

A suspicion finally slid into her mind. 'You can't…' she whispered, appalled yet fascinated, and excited when he pushed her legs apart and lowered his head to her feminine core.

'Want to bet on it?'

His accent was thicker than usual, and his breath fanned the sensitive skin on her inner thigh. One strong hand curled around her ankle. He lifted her leg and draped it over his shoulder. And then he simply put his mouth against her centre and ran his tongue over her opening, making the ache she felt there so much worse, so much *more*.

Juliet glanced down at his dark head between her thighs and knew there was a part of her that was horrified for allowing him to pleasure her in such a way. But she could not deny that he was giving her the most exquisite pleasure as he teased and tormented her with his tongue. She sank back against the mattress, twisting her head from side to side as the heat and the fire and the terrible need inside her built to a crescendo.

Nothing had prepared her for sheer delight of Rafael's intimate caresses, or his soft murmurs of approval when she arched her hips and offered herself to him. She was aware of a coiling sensation low in her pelvis that wound tighter and tighter, until she was trembling and desperate for something that hovered frustratingly out of reach.

And then it happened.

He flicked his tongue across the tight nub of her clitoris and the coil inside her snapped, sending starbursts of pleasure shooting out from her core in a series of exquisite spasms that made her internal muscles clench and release, clench and release, flooding her with the sticky sweetness of her earth-shattering climax.

Her first.

She would remember it long after their marriage was over.

Her heart contracted painfully as the thought slid like a serpent in paradise into her mind.

In the aftermath, as her breathing slowed, she realised that the most amazing sexual experience of her life could not have been satisfactory for Rafael. When he leaned over her and kissed her lingeringly on her mouth she tasted her own feminine sweetness on his lips and wondered if he expected her to afford him the same pleasure he had given her. But how to suggest it?

She felt frustrated by her inexperience. 'I—' She broke off, at a loss to know what to say. He had taken her apart utterly and she didn't know how to put herself back together again, or if she even could.

She watched him uncertainly when he stepped away from the bed. 'I can hear Poppy,' he murmured.

Her daughter! How could she have forgotten?

She scrambled off the bed when she heard voices from somewhere in the apartment and guessed that Sofia had returned Poppy after she'd spent the afternoon with the twins.

'I'll go and see her while you get dressed,' Rafael said, kissing the tip of her nose before he strolled out of the room.

It took Juliet seconds to slip into the blue silk dress she had worn at lunch. Silently cursing the tell-tale flush on her cheeks, she hurried through the apartment.

As she entered the sitting room Poppy ran towards her. 'Mummy, can I have my pyjamas?'

'It's not bedtime.'

Sofia laughed. 'The twins would like Poppy to come to us for a sleepover.' She glanced at her brother. 'Rafael has explained that you have a dinner engagement in Valencia this evening, so it's perfect timing.'

It was the first Juliet had heard of a dinner engagement, but Rafael seemed determined to avoid her gaze.

For the next ten minutes she was busy packing a bag with Poppy's pyjamas, toothbrush and an assortment of cuddly toys. She gave her daughter a big hug and felt a pang when Poppy trotted off happily with Sofia. Her baby was growing up so fast.

When they had gone she turned to Rafael. 'Who are we meeting? Some more of your relatives? Or is it a business dinner?' She did not relish the thought of either. 'What should I wear?' She frowned when he didn't answer. 'Is it a formal function?'

'It's a date.'

'A *date*?' Her confusion grew as dull colour ran along his cheekbones. 'I don't understand.'

'It's quite simple, *chiquita*,' he said, strolling towards her. 'I'm taking you to dinner, away from the Casillas mansion, so that we can spend some time alone.'

'I thought the point was for us to stay here in the house under your grandfather's nose so that we can convince him our marriage is real?'

Instead of replying, Rafael tucked a tendril of hair that had escaped from her chignon behind her ear. The unexpectedly tender gesture tugged on Juliet's heart.

'I would like to explore the attraction between us and I think you would like to do that too,' he said quietly.

She did not deny it and a heavy sigh escaped him.

'We have done everything in the wrong order—married before we had even spent a day together. I was arrogant enough to believe that it didn't matter. But I would like us to start again. So, *bella Julieta*, will you have dinner with me?'

She nodded, feeling suddenly shy, but excited too—and apprehensive, and a host of other emotions she was afraid to define. Rafael had made it clear that he desired her, and although it felt as if she was about to jump from the top of a precipice she was ready to leap into the unknown.

'I'd love to.'

'Good.' He dropped a swift, hard kiss on her mouth that left her lips tingling. 'I have some work to do in my study and we'll leave in an hour.' He paused on his way out of the room. 'By the way, you'll need to bring an overnight bag as we'll be spending the night at my penthouse in the city. Oh, and wear something sexy, *amante*.'

Juliet's heart missed a beat. *Amante* meant lover.

# CHAPTER NINE

'WE COULD SKIP dinner and go straight to the penthouse.'

Rafael's voice was oddly hoarse and it sent a shiver across Juliet's skin. She tore her gaze from the unholy gleam in his eyes and glanced around the restaurant, which he'd told her was one of the best places to eat in Valencia. Situated in a charming little square in the old part of the city, it had plenty of atmosphere, and a band was playing traditional Spanish music.

He had promised her a date. 'I'm hungry,' she told him, unfolding her napkin.

'Same here,' he growled. 'You look incredible in that dress. Good enough to eat.' His accent thickened. 'I am looking forward to tasting you again later.'

Heat scorched her cheeks at the memory of how he had pleasured her with his tongue, and she buried her face in her menu. A black velvet dress clung to her slender figure and the low-cut neckline pushed her breasts up to give her a cleavage. Sheer black stockings and high-heeled strappy sandals completed the outfit, and she had left her hair loose, with just the front sections drawn back from her face with diamante clips.

She'd worn a lightweight wool coat when they had left the Casillas mansion, so Rafael had only seen her dress when they'd arrived at the restaurant. The sizzling look he'd given her had made her feel like a sex goddess and boosted her confidence.

When the waiter had taken their order Juliet sipped her champagne cocktail and gave a small sigh. None of this was real. She still expected to wake up in her flat in the tower block and find it had all been a dream. Especially Rafael.

Her eyes were drawn across the table to him. In tailored black trousers and a black silk shirt, casually open at the throat to reveal a vee of bronzed skin, he was darkly gorgeous, and the black stubble on his jaw gave him a dangerous sexiness that sent her heart clattering against her ribs.

'Were you in love with Poppy's father?'

Startled by his question, she gave him a wry look. 'I thought I was. I met him at a party given by some friends of my cousin. Bryan was good-looking, and he knew it, and I was naïve and grieving for my parents. I was flattered that he'd noticed me. But after we'd slept together he told me he'd only wanted sex.'

She sighed.

'I had been taking the contraceptive pill to regulate my periods, and I stupidly agreed to have sex with him without a condom. I'd been taking a herbal remedy to help with my feelings of depression following my parents' deaths and I had no idea that it could decrease the effectiveness of the pill. When I discovered I was pregnant Bryan wasn't interested, and he refused to support his child, although he did agree to have his name on Poppy's birth certificate.'

'He sounds like a jerk. It's Bryan's responsibility to make a financial contribution towards his daughter's upbringing.'

Juliet stared at Rafael. 'Would you support *your* child? You're a renowned playboy, but if one of your mistresses became pregnant what would *you* do?'

'It won't happen because I always use protection,' he told her smoothly. Seeing her frown, he added, 'But in the extremely unlikely event that it did, I would make a settlement to ensure the child had financial security for life.'

She grimaced. 'Money isn't everything. A child needs to be loved and nurtured. My parents had little money but I had a wonderfully happy childhood, with the security of knowing they loved me.'

'I had a miserable childhood, living in poverty—and, believe me, money would have made a huge difference to my life and my sister's.' A nerve flickered in Rafael's cheek. 'The best thing—no, the *only* thing I could give a child of mine is access to my wealth.'

His harsh tone warned Juliet to drop a subject that was clearly contentious, but she couldn't. 'Are you saying you wouldn't want to be involved in your child's life? You wouldn't *love* your child?'

'The question is irrelevant,' he said coldly.

His expression was as haughty as his mother's, Juliet thought. Centuries of his family's aristocratic heritage were stamped on his hard features and revealed that he was every bit a

Casillas. No doubt some of his noble ancestors had been as ruthless as Rafael was.

It was a relief when the waiter arrived at their table to serve the first course. When they were alone again Juliet stayed silent while she ate her grilled scallops with chorizo. The food was delicious, but tears pricked the back of her eyes at the thought that she had spoiled the evening.

Rafael sipped his wine. 'I thought you might like to visit the Museum of Fine Arts tomorrow. The building is very beautiful, and worth visiting simply to see the baroque architecture. It houses the second most important art collection in Spain.'

'I'd love to go.'

His mention of 'tomorrow' reminded her that they would be staying at his apartment in the city tonight.

'But what about Poppy? I'll need to get back for her.'

'My sister is planning to take all three girls to the beach, and she will have the nanny to help out. Valencia is a beautiful city and I think you would enjoy the City of Arts and Sciences and the aquarium—although both are a day's visit. But we don't have to do everything in one day. There will be plenty of time in the year ahead for you to enjoy all that Valencia has to offer.'

Rafael's words were a timely reminder of why she was there with him. Their marriage was a temporary arrangement and she would be a fool to hope for more than he was offering.

Why not use this opportunity to explore her sensuality and enjoy great sex, free from the expectations that came with a normal relationship? Juliet asked herself while the waiter cleared away her plate and served her main course. Life had taught her to seize the moment, and she would regret it for ever if she did not make love with Rafael. As long as she remembered that *love* wasn't involved.

She looked up, and her heart leapt when she found him watching her. His mouth crooked in a sexy smile that made her pulse race and her spirits soar as the awkwardness between them disappeared. For the rest of the meal they chatted with an ease that surprised her. Rafael had travelled widely and she was fascinated to hear of the places he had visited.

'I've only been to Australia—and now Spain,' she admitted.

'I have to go to New York for a few days next month. I'll take you with me.'

Going to New York was another dream of hers that she had never imagined she would fulfil when she had lived in the tower block.

Juliet licked the last morsel of the chocolate mousse she had chosen for dessert from her spoon. The light-as-air mousse felt sensual on her tongue and she closed her eyes while she enjoyed the sensory experience.

'*Dios...*' Rafael growled. 'Do you do that on purpose?'

Her eyes flew open. 'Do what?' she asked innocently.

Instead of replying, he dipped his spoon into his own dish of mousse and leaned across the table to hold the loaded spoon against her lips. 'You would tempt a saint, *bella*, and piety is not my strong point. Open your mouth,' he ordered softly.

Juliet could not resist the rich mousse, or Rafael, and she obediently parted her lips and licked the dessert from his spoon. He made a thick sound in his throat that provoked a flood of molten warmth between her legs.

She watched him dip the spoon back into his bowl and then lift it to his own mouth. She could not tear her gaze from his tongue as he licked his spoon clean. It was incredibly erotic, and heat coiled through her as she imagined him using that wicked tongue on her body.

She swallowed, searching her mind for something—anything—to say that would break the sexual tension that crackled between them.

'I've heard this music before,' she murmured, recognising the tune that the band were playing. 'My uncle Carlos is a brilliant acoustic guitarist and he used to play this.'

Rafael pushed back his chair and stood up. 'Dance with me,' he said, holding out his hand to her. 'This music is flamenco. It originated in the gypsy communities in southern Spain and is as fiery and passionate as the people who created it.'

Dazedly Juliet put her hand in his and allowed him to lead her to the small dance floor in the centre of the restaurant, where a few other couples were already dancing. Rafael drew her into his arms and placed one hand in the small of her back, holding her so that her pelvis was pressed up against his. A tremor ran through her when she felt the bulge of his arousal through his trousers.

He danced with a natural grace and Juliet matched his rhythm, swaying her hips in time with his as the dance became a seduction of her senses. Nothing existed but the music and this man whose green eyes gleamed with a naked hunger as he lowered his head towards her, compelling her to slide her hand around his neck and pull his mouth down to hers.

She was drowning in the whirlpool of sensations that he was creating with his mouth as he plundered her lips in a kiss that left her trembling. He threaded his fingers through her hair while he trailed hot kisses along her jaw. Need clawed inside her, obliterating every sane thought and leaving a kind of madness, a wild restlessness that only Rafael could assuage.

And all the while they danced together to the music of the flamenco as the tempo quickened and became more intense.

'We need to leave,' he growled close to her ear.

Minutes later he'd settled the bill and escorted her out of the restaurant to where his car was parked. Neither of them spoke on the short journey to his city apartment. The sexual tension in the car and then in the lift on the way up to the penthouse was tangible, and Juliet's heart pounded as Rafael leaned against the wall of the lift and studied her with a brooding intensity.

The penthouse was ultra-modern and stylish. A bachelor pad, Juliet thought as she took in the pale wood floors, white leather sofas and colourful modern art on the walls of the open-plan living space. She bit her lip as she wondered how many of his mistresses he had brought here.

'Would you like to take a look around the apartment?' Rafael offered, standing behind her to take her coat when she slipped it off her shoulders.

She felt his hand smooth her hair. 'Not really,' she said huskily.

'Can I get you a drink?'

'No, thank you.'

He placed her coat over the back of a chair and came to stand in front of her, his glittering gaze making her stomach swoop. 'What *would* you like, *chiquita*?'

'You.'

The word burst from her. She couldn't help it. He had driven her crazy with longing all evening with every smile he'd sent her as they had lingered over conversation and champagne— flirting with her, she realised.

He laughed, and the sound filled her with golden light and a fire that burned hotter still when he opened his arms wide.

'Have me, then, *bella Julieta*.'

His laughter stole around her as she literally threw herself into his waiting arms and he lifted her off her feet.

'Wrap your legs around me,' he told her, and when she obeyed he gave a groan as her pelvis pressed hard against his arousal.

He carried her into the bedroom and set her down next to the bed. She was vaguely conscious of muted lighting and décor of black and gold, a printed throw on the bed. But then he bent his head to claim her mouth and she was only conscious of Rafael: the slide of his lips over hers, the heady scent of his cologne mixed with the indefinable musk of male pheromones, the heat of his body beneath her palms as she ran her hands over his chest and tugged open his shirt buttons.

He undressed her, taking his time to slide her zip down her spine and peel her dress away from her breasts, baring her to his hot gaze. But he didn't touch her breasts yet, focusing instead on tugging her tight-fitting dress over her hips so that it fell to the floor and she stepped out of it.

*'Dios,'* he said roughly as he stared at her sheer black stockings. 'If I'd known you were wearing these…' he traced his fingers over the wide bands of lace around the tops of her thighs '…we wouldn't have made it past the starter.'

He knelt to remove her shoes and then slowly drew one stocking down her leg, then the other, pressing his lips along her white scar, his gentle kisses healing the deeper scars inside her.

'You are so beautiful,' he murmured, and there was nothing but truth and hunger in his eyes when he stood and drew her into his arms.

He made her feel beautiful. And, oh, he made her want him when he kissed her as if he could not have enough of her, when he cupped her breasts in his palms and stroked his thumbs over her nipples so that they peaked and she shuddered beneath the pleasure of his touch.

His hands skimmed down to her panties and he hooked his fingers in the waistband to draw them down her legs.

'So beautiful,' he said again, his low tone aching with need, making the ache between her legs even more acute.

He stripped with an efficiency that caused her a tiny flicker of doubt. Rafael had done this a thousand times or more—perhaps he would be disappointed by her inexperience. But then he took off his boxer shorts, and the sight of his erection jutting so big and bold turned her insides to liquid.

Did he see the flash of uncertainty in her eyes when she viewed the awesome size of him?

He slipped his hand beneath her chin and tilted her face to his. 'We'll take things slowly, *cariño*,' he promised, rubbing his thumb across her lower lip. And then he lay down on the bed and pulled her on top of him, arranging her so that she sat astride him and the hard ridge of his arousal was *there*, pressing against her opening.

But he didn't push any further forward, and it was his finger that stroked over her moist vagina, gently parting her and easing inside her, swirling and twisting, making her gasp and rock her hips against his hand. A second finger joined the first, testing her, stretching her, while his other hand cradled her breast and he tugged her down so that he could close his lips around her nipple and suck hard, so that she gave a moan and molten heat pooled between her legs.

Juliet pushed herself upright and ran her hands greedily over his torso, loving the feel of his satin skin and the faint abrasion of his chest hair beneath her palms.

'Kiss me,' he ordered, and all that arrogance of his was there in his gravelly voice and in his eyes that gleamed fiercely beneath his half-closed eyelids.

She did not hesitate—simply placed her hands flat on the bed on either side of his head and lowered her mouth to his. He might be arrogant but he wanted her—badly—and she kissed him with all her passion and need, with all her heart and soul, because she was intrinsically honest and her lips could not lie as they clung to his.

'*Querida...*' he groaned, and set her away from him while he reached across to the bedside drawer and took out a condom.

She watched him roll it down his hard length and her heart hammered in her chest, anticipation and the faintest apprehension causing her to catch her breath.

His gaze sought hers and she was entranced by the darkness of desire that had turned his green eyes almost black. She read the unspoken question in his eyes and her breath escaped her on a soft sigh of assent.

He lifted her into position above him and then pulled her slowly down so that his erection nudged her opening. Holding her hips, he guided her, his eyes locked with hers as his swollen tip stretched her and pressed deeper, deeper, filling her inch by inch, and it was so impossibly intense that she thought she would die in the beauty of his possession.

The feel of Rafael inside her was perfect— beyond anything she could have imagined as he began to move, thrusting into her with steady strokes while he slipped his hands round to cup her bottom. His head was thrown back against the pillows, his black hair falling across his brow, his eyes blazing into hers.

'Dance for me,' he said thickly.

And she did. Catching his rhythm, she closed her eyes and lost herself in the magic of an age-old dance, arching her supple body above him, throwing her head back as they moved together in total accord and flew ever upwards towards the pinnacle.

It couldn't last. Fire this bright had to burn out.

The power of him moving inside her stole her breath and the perfection of each devastating thrust broke her heart. This was not just sex. Not for her. Deep down, she'd known it would be more, that *making love* with Rafael was exactly what she was doing.

She leaned forward so that her nipples brushed across his chest, making him groan and increase his pace. She kissed his mouth and her heart flipped when he pushed his tongue between her lips. The storm was about to break and she arched her body backwards, shaking her hair over her shoulders as the pressure built deep in her pelvis.

'*Dios*, what you do to me...' he muttered—raw, harsh, as if the words were torn from him.

His jaw was clenched and she sensed he was fighting for control—a battle he lost spectacularly when he exploded inside her at the same moment that she shattered. Her sharp cry mingled with his deep groan as they rode out the storm together, and she felt the flooding sweetness of her orgasm and heard the uneven rasp of his laboured breaths.

In the aftermath she lay sprawled across his chest, too exhilarated, too empowered, too *everything* to be able to move. But the idea that he would think she was clingy and needy finally stirred her and she attempted to roll off him—only for him to tighten his arms around her.

'Stay.'

The word rumbled through his chest and tugged on Juliet's heart. She heard in his low tone the boy who had been abandoned by his mother. She heard the teenager shunned by his rich relatives because they believed his background was shameful, when it was they who should have been ashamed.

*Don't*, she told her heart sternly when it leapt at the feel of his hand stroking her hair. She must not allow the idea that Rafael was in any way vulnerable to breach her defences.

But when he rolled them both over so that she was beneath him, and he sought her mouth in a kiss of beguiling sweetness and the renewed flowering of passion, she knew that the warning was too late.

Something had changed and now Rafael knew it was him. It had started when he had told Juliet about his boyhood, which he had never spoken of to anyone—not even to Tio Alvaro, to whom he was closest out of all his relatives.

But perhaps it had started before that—when he had watched Juliet descend the stairs at his grandfather's birthday party, a vision of ethereal loveliness in that golden dress.

*His wife.*

He wasn't comfortable with the possessive feeling that swept through him, nor did he understand it. Rafael knew what he was—knew better than to think he could be a better man.

The kind of man a woman might love. It was hardly likely when his own mother hadn't loved him and his father had used any excuse to beat the life out of him. A few times he had very nearly succeeded.

Rafael hated the name Mendoza, but he'd kept it because it reminded him of what he was—what he feared he could be. Tacking Casillas on to his name did not make him a member of the family, his grandfather had told him more than once. Which meant that he was no one—nothing.

Why, suddenly, did it matter? Why did he care? And, even worse, why did she wish that he could overcome the legacy of his past?

The answer to those questions circling like vultures in his mind was curled up beside him, sleeping as only the innocent could sleep, with her hand tucked under her cheek and her lips slightly parted so that when he put his face close to hers her sweet breath whispered across his skin.

It astonished him that he had once thought her plain. He wondered if she'd felt victorious when he'd come so hard inside her, three times the previous night, that his groans had echoed around the bedroom. Now the pearly grey light of dawn filled the room, and the only way to resist the temptation to pull her beneath him again was to get out of bed.

Juliet needed to sleep after he'd kept her awake for much of the night with his demands—which she had enjoyed, he reminded himself as he pulled on a pair of sweatpants. They were mercifully loose around his erection, which had sprung to attention when he'd pushed back the sheet and unintentionally exposed one of Juliet's pale breasts, tipped with a nipple that was rosy red from the ministrations of his mouth.

Rafael walked through the penthouse and made a jug of coffee. Then he stood in front of the glass doors and watched the sun rise over Valencia. Nothing had changed, he decided. He felt in control of himself once more as the caffeine entered his bloodstream. In a year he would achieve his goal of becoming CEO, and by then his fascination with Juliet would have faded. Desire was always transient, but for now she was his.

He shoved a hand through his hair, remembering her hungry little cries when they'd shared a bath last night and he'd made her come as he'd eased his long fingers inside her. Never before had he taken such delight in giving a woman pleasure. Juliet's curious mix of innocence and heart-stopping sensuality intrigued him.

'Rafael?'

Her voice sounded from behind him and he turned, frowning when he saw her wary expression, the vulnerability that she successfully hid from most people but not from him.

'I woke up and you'd gone, and I thought...'

She'd thought he had used her for a night of sex, in the same way that the father of her child had done.

Rafael did not question why he felt a tugging sensation beneath his breastbone. He simply strode across the room and pulled her into his arms. 'I'm an early riser,' he said lightly, aware of another tug in his chest when relief flashed in her eyes.

That's very apparent,' she murmured drily, moving her hand over the tell-tale bulge beneath his sweatpants.

He laughed. He couldn't help it. And it felt so good, so carefree, that he laughed again as he scooped her into his arms and carried her back to the bedroom.

Her impish smile stole his breath. 'Are we going back to bed? Because I've had enough sleep...'

'Who said anything about sleeping, *chiquita*?'

# CHAPTER TEN

'WHERE ARE YOU GOING?'

Rafael's gravelly voice halted Juliet's attempt to wriggle over to the edge of the bed. They were in the bedroom of his private suite at the Casillas mansion. It was a huge bed, and for the past few weeks she hadn't slept in it alone. His stretched out his arm and hauled her back across the mattress.

'I was trying not to wake you,' she mumbled, pressing her face against his warm chest and listening to the steady thud of his heart.

'I've been awake for a while.' He chuckled. 'Did you really think I would remain asleep while you were taking liberties with my body, *querida*?'

'Oh.'

She burrowed closer to him to hide her hot face. She'd had no idea that Rafael had been aware when she'd pulled back the sheet and made a detailed study of his naked body with her eyes and hands. He was a work of art: lean and yet powerfully muscular, his bronzed skin overlaid with black hair that arrowed over his flat stomach and down to his impressive manhood.

'I'd like to know what you intend to do about *this* as you're responsible for it,' he drawled, flipping her over onto her back and settling himself between her thighs so that his rockhard erection jabbed her belly.

'I was going to make coffee,' she said breathlessly. 'Don't you have to get up for work?'

'I'll go into the office late.'

'But you're coming back early for the twins' birthday party,' she reminded him, catching her breath when Rafael flicked his tongue across a turgid nipple.

'Mmm… There has definitely been a drop in my productivity since I married you.'

'I have no complaints about your performance,' she said, and gasped as she wrapped her legs around his hips and he surged into her.

He grinned and her heart contracted. She loved it when he smiled, and lately he'd smiled a lot. *She loved him*, whispered a voice inside her, but Juliet didn't want to admit that dangerous truth to herself, let alone to Rafael.

Much later, after they had shared a shower and he'd given her another bone-melting orgasm while she'd been bent over the side of the bath, he finally went to work. It was lucky that Poppy now slept in the nursery with Sofia's twins, Juliet mused as she stepped onto the balcony and found her daughter eating breakfast with the nanny.

Poppy had formed a real bond with Elvira, as she had with Sofia and Ana and Inez. It would be a wrench when she took Poppy back to live in England.

The thought sent Juliet's heart hurtling down to her toes. She had never imagined when Rafael had brought her to the Casillas mansion that she could be this happy and feel so settled. Some of his relatives had been cool towards her at first, but others, like his aunt Lucia and uncle Alvaro, were friendly and made a fuss of Poppy.

Rafael's mother had kept her distance since that explosive lunch, but Juliet didn't regret the things she'd said to Delfina. Rafael had told her more about his terrible childhood in the slum, and Sofia had also spoken to her about their early life.

'I don't remember much about the slum or my father,' she'd told Juliet. 'My brother took care of me and I felt safe with him.'

But no one had taken care of Rafael and protected him from his violent father—least of all his mother, who had abandoned him and then spurned him, or his grandfather, who had found him but refused to acknowledge Rafael as his successor.

Juliet knew she must not forget the reason why Rafael had married her, but over the past weeks she had felt closer to him than she'd ever felt to another person. Even though she had adored her parents and known they loved her, their love for each other had come first. But it would be the worst folly to start believing that Rafael was hers, or that he too felt a connection between them that went beyond the passion they shared.

Pushing her complicated thoughts to the back of her mind, she sat down at the table with Poppy and Elvira and poured herself a cup of coffee. A feeling of nausea swept over her and she set her cup down without taking a sip. She was probably hungry, she decided. But the sick feeling grew worse after she'd eaten some yoghurt and she hoped she wasn't coming down with another gastric virus.

Luckily the sensation of nausea soon passed, and she spent the morning at the pool with Poppy before Elvira took the little girl back to the house for lunch.

Juliet was aware that Rafael's grandfather had come to sit beneath a parasol on the pool terrace. She had barely spoken to him since he had been so unpleasant to her when Rafael had introduced her as his wife, but she had left her book on the table where Hector was now sitting.

Steeling herself for more of his rudeness, she walked over to him, puzzled to see two copies of a psychological thriller by a popular author on the table.

'Are you enjoying the book?' she asked as she picked up her copy.

Hector shrugged. 'It is good, but I have not read very much of it. My eyesight is poor because I have cataracts in my eyes which impair my vision. A surgical procedure could resolve the problem, but I also suffer from a heart condition and my doctor has advised me against having an anaesthetic.'

'I'm sorry. You must find it frustrating not to be able to read. I know I would.' Juliet hesitated. 'I could read to you, if you like.'

After a moment he nodded, and said rather stiffly. 'Do you have time? Your little daughter keeps you busy.'

'Oh, Poppy will have a nap after lunch.' Juliet picked up Hector's copy of the thriller and opened it at the page he had bookmarked. 'It's lucky this is the English edition. I'm not very good at reading in Spanish.'

'But you speak the language fluently.' He sighed. 'I must apologise for the reception you received when my grandson brought you here.'

Juliet was not one to hold a grudge. 'That's all right. I wasn't what you were expecting. I'm not the kind of wife you hoped Rafael would marry.'

'No,' Hector admitted. 'But I have watched you with Rafael and I think you are a good wife to him. You love him, don't you?'

She flushed. Were her feelings for Rafael so obvious? If so, had he guessed how she felt about him?

She met his grandfather's knowing gaze. 'Yes,' she said huskily.

It occurred to her that she was supposed to be trying to convince Hector that their marriage was genuine, but she didn't have to pretend that she had feelings for Rafael.

She looked down at the book in her hand. 'Chapter Four...' she began.

The Valencian sun grew hotter as the summer progressed, and Juliet spent much of her time slathering sun cream on herself and Poppy, cursing their pale Anglo Saxon skin that burned so easily. Even so she had developed a light golden tan, and Poppy brimmed with energy and had learned to swim without water aids.

Life couldn't get much better than this, she thought one afternoon. A few days ago she had received a letter from the Australian law firm informing her that Bryan was no longer seeking custody of Poppy.

The reason he'd given for dropping his claim was that he felt reassured that Poppy was now growing up in a stable family environment since Juliet's marriage. But her cousin in Sydney had heard that Bryan's heiress girlfriend had dumped him. Juliet had emailed, offering Bryan phone contact with his daughter, and possibly visits when Poppy was older, but she'd had no response.

It was a huge relief to know she would not lose Poppy. She looked over at where the little girl was busy building a sandcastle. They had spent the day at the Casillas estate's private beach—her, Rafael and Poppy, and Sofia, her husband Marcus and the twins. They had swum in sea that was as warm as a bath, and now the men were tending to a barbecue while the children played and she and Sofia had a chance to relax.

They must look like a typical family group, Juliet thought, looking over at Rafael and finding him staring at her. Their eyes met, held, and he smiled, his teeth flashing white in his tanned face, causing her heart to skip a beat.

It was tempting to believe that it was all real: the lingering looks he gave her when she glanced up from her book, his smile which was the first thing she saw when she opened her eyes every morning, the way he held her close after sex. And the sex… She bit her lip, thankful that her sarong hid the hard nipples jutting beneath her bikini top as she remembered how he had made love to her on this very beach the previous evening, after they had walked hand in hand along the shoreline at sunset and he'd tumbled her down onto the sand.

Rafael had told her that he would not fall in love with her. He didn't believe in love, only lust. But was it foolish to think, to hope, that he might see her as more than his public wife and private mistress?

Juliet sighed as her mind turned to the niggling worry that had the potential to shatter the fairy tale. Her period was late. Only by a few days, but it was enough for her to feel concerned. It had got her thinking about her period last month, which had been unusually light. She'd put it down to the gastric virus she'd had when she'd arrived in Spain. The feeling of nausea when she smelled coffee was another red light, but it was probably all in her imagination.

To put her mind at rest she'd bought a pregnancy test, and if her period didn't start in another couple of days she would take it. She closed her eyes and an image popped into her mind of a chubby olive-skinned baby with a mop of black hair and green eyes like his father's.

Startled, she jerked upright and blinked at Rafael as he dropped down onto the sand beside her.

'You fell asleep in the sun,' he murmured, brushing his lips across hers in a lingering kiss. 'What's the matter, *querida*, did you have a bad dream?'

She swallowed. 'Something like that.'

'Well, Madre, what is this about?'

Rafael did not hide his impatience. He didn't want to be cooling his heels in his mother's cushion-stuffed sitting room when Juliet was waiting for him in his own apartment. Hopefully she would already be in bed, but if not he would soon take her there.

An early-morning meeting meant that he'd left for the office before Juliet had woken up. Usually they had sex first thing, and he'd missed it—missed *her*, if he cared to admit it. Which he did not.

'I want to talk to you.' Delfina was twisting

her hands together and seemed hesitant. 'When you brought your wife to lunch…it must be three months ago now… I told you that I was ashamed, and you assumed that I meant I was ashamed of *you*.'

'An easy assumption to make as you have barely been able to look at me for the past twenty-three years,' he said sardonically.

'I was ashamed of myself. I *am* ashamed of what I did to you,' Delfina whispered. 'When Juliet accused me of abandoning you, leaving you with your violent father, I saw the condemnation in her eyes and knew I deserved it. I knew what Ivan was like…the monster he was.'

She sighed.

'I had led a sheltered life and he was dangerously attractive. Within months of running away with him he'd persuaded me to take drugs. It was his way of controlling me, and as my life with him spiralled ever downwards I took more drugs to block out the grim reality of life with him.'

Delfina dropped her face into her hands.

'I don't even remember giving birth to you

or your sister. I felt half alive. But then one day I saw my father on the television and all I wanted was to go back to my *papà*, who had always protected me. I took some money out of Ivan's wallet and somehow I made it back to my family.'

'*I* was your family,' Rafael said harshly. 'Me and Sofia. Your *children*. And you left us with him.'

His mother was crying. He had never seen her cry before and he was angry that her tears hurt him. She hadn't cared about *him*.

'I was afraid of him.'

'Do you think *I* wasn't? You called him a monster and that's exactly what the man who fathered me was.' A monster whose blood ran through *his* veins, Rafael thought, and something bleak and hopeless lashed his heart.

'I'm sorry,' his mother sobbed. 'I know you must hate me. I never knew how to try and reach out to you. When Hector brought you here you were so angry. And as you grew older you were cold and hard, and I knew it was my fault that you never smiled with your eyes.' Delfina took a shaky breath. 'This girl you've married...'

'Juliet,' Rafael gritted. 'My wife's name is Juliet.'

'She is a brave young woman,' his mother said quietly. 'She is good for you. She makes you smile.'

Delfina put her hand on Rafael's arm. It was the first time they'd had any sort of physical contact since— He frowned, unable to remember a time when his mother had touched him, let alone hugged him, unlike Juliet, who constantly hugged and cuddled her daughter.

'Rafael, I am reaching out now,' Delfina said in a trembling voice. 'I cannot expect you to forgive me, but I wish that some day we can be...friends.'

He should tell his mother to get lost and walk away. A few months ago he probably would have done, Rafael acknowledged. But life was short, as Juliet often said. Juliet, his wife, who had more courage in her tiny body than the tallest giant. Right now he didn't know if he could forgive his mother, but he found that he didn't want to walk away, so he placed his hand over Delfina's and gently squeezed her fingers.

'It's all right, Madre.'

\* \* \*

Juliet did much more than make him smile, Rafael thought, recalling his mother's words as he entered his apartment. Juliet intrigued him, fascinated him, drove him crazy with her stubbornness and evoked an ache inside him that defied explanation when he watched her with her little daughter. She was an amazing mother and an amazing lover, and if he was a different man he might have hoped for things that he'd long ago accepted he could never have.

But he could not escape his past. He could not be a different man. So he would settle for having her in his bed, and if the nine months that were left of their marriage seemed not enough—not nearly enough—he would bury that thought and live for the day, which was how he had survived his childhood.

He found her standing outside on the balcony. She was wearing a simple white dress made of a floaty material that skimmed over her slender figure like gossamer, and her hair was loose, falling down her back like a river of amber silk.

'There you are,' he said, and there was satisfaction in his voice as he thought of the evening ahead and an early dinner and an early night—not necessarily in that order.

He waited for her to turn around and give him one of her smiles that lit up her face and did something peculiar to his heart rate.

But she seemed to stiffen before she swung round, and she didn't smile. Her eyes were very blue—as blue as the summer sky.

'I have something to tell you.'

Out of nowhere Rafael felt sick with dread. It was the same feeling he'd had when he was a boy and he'd heard the swish of his father's belt. The hairs on the back of his neck prickled with foreboding.

'So tell me,' he said evenly, while his heart thudded.

Juliet lifted a hand and let it fall to her side again. 'I'm pregnant.'

Silence. So intense it pressed on him. And then a roaring in his ears.

Every muscle in his body clenched in rejection of something that he knew from her face was true. But he rejected it anyway. 'You can't be. We've always been careful. Even on the goddamned beach I made sure I had condoms in my pocket.'

'It was before then.'

She swallowed and he saw her slender throat convulse.

'The test shows that I'm nine weeks.'

He shook his head. 'That's more than two months. How didn't you know before?'

Not that it mattered, Rafael thought grimly, turning away from her and gripping the balustrade before his legs gave out. Juliet was expecting his baby. *Dios.* How could *he* be a father? The son of a monster? He'd decided long ago that his bloodline—the Mendoza bloodline—had to end with him.

'I know it's not what you had planned,' she said in a low voice.

He closed his eyes as her words struck him another blow. *What he had planned.* A fake marriage so that he could claim the CEO-ship. His arrogance mocked him and he felt ashamed of the ambition that was all he had, all he was.

He knew what he had to do. For Juliet's sake and for the child she carried. Especially for the child's sake.

'No,' he said unemotionally. 'A baby was not in my plans nor what I wished for.'

'Here's a newsflash, Rafael. Your wishes no longer matter.'

The bite in her voice made him turn his head and he saw anger on her face—and something else…something fiercely protective. A lioness defending her cub, he realised, and admiration joined the swirling mix of emotions he was trying to control.

'Like it or not, I am going to have your baby.'

He nodded and turned away from her again, to stare unseeingly across the gardens to the sea beyond. When this was done he would go for a run along the beach, but he knew he wouldn't be able to outrun his demons. They would sit on his shoulders, terrible and ugly, reminding him of why he dared not deal with this situation differently. Why his child and Juliet would be safer without him.

'I will ask my lawyers to begin divorce proceedings,' he told her flatly. 'Spanish law allows couples to seek a no-blame divorce after three months of marriage, a fact of which my grandfather is unaware. And I'll make immediate arrangements for you and Poppy to return to England. Ferndown House will be made over to you and five million pounds transferred into your bank account as per our agreement. I will also make further provision for Poppy and the child you are carrying.'

'*Your* child,' Juliet said fiercely. 'I am carrying *your* child.'

Rafael felt the glare she sent him but he didn't look at her, and after a moment she gave a heavy sigh.

'You know we can't divorce until we have been married for a year—your grandfather insisted on that before he will make you CEO.'

'Then I won't be CEO.'

If he allowed her to live at the Casillas mansion until their first wedding anniversary he would see her body change as her pregnancy progressed and he'd be tempted to hope for a miracle. If she was already two months pregnant the child would be born seven months from now, but their marriage had nine months to run, which meant that some sort of involvement with his child would be unavoidable. He couldn't risk it.

Juliet's silence compelled Rafael to look at her. He watched the tears roll down her face and hardened his heart. She would never know how much it was costing him to send her away.

He was only just starting to realise that despite his best efforts to avoid this kind of situation, this level of pain, he had been reckless when he'd allowed Juliet close. All he could do now was try to limit the damage.

'Do you hate the idea of having a child so much that you're willing to give up your claim to be your grandfather's successor and head of the Casillas Group?'

Juliet stared at him, and when she spoke again her voice was cold—as cold as the ice around his heart.

'In that case the baby will be better off without any father rather than growing up with a father who does not love him.'

Rafael's jaw clenched and despite himself he was curious. 'Him? You know it's a boy?'

'It's too early for a scan to show the baby's gender, but I am sure I'm having a boy.' She reached out her hand towards him and let it fall again. 'Rafael... It doesn't have to be like this. I understand if you don't want me. That you might feel trapped—' Her voice cracked. 'But your son needs his father.'

'And what if I am my father's son?' he said harshly. 'No child needs a father like mine.'

He saw shock on Juliet's face, confusion. The wounded expression in her eyes felt like an arrow through Rafael's heart. He did not trust himself to be near her and without another word he walked away.

# CHAPTER ELEVEN

JULIET CURLED UP in a tight ball in the bed that was much too big for her alone and cried until her head hurt and her eyes burned. Some time around dawn she slept fitfully, and when she woke she cried again because Rafael's head wasn't on the pillow beside her, He wasn't there to greet her with a smile that promised it would be another beautiful day.

Maybe there would never be another beautiful day. Just grey, sad days, like the days and weeks and months after that lorry had wiped out everything she'd cared about when she was a teenager.

She stumbled into the bathroom and splashed water on her puffy face. All that crying had made her look like a frog. It was lucky there was no chance that Rafael would see her.

He hadn't come back to the apartment after he'd stormed out the previous night, but he'd sent her a text telling her that he had gone to his penthouse in Valencia and would arrange for the Casillas private jet to take her and Poppy back to London.

More tears came into her eyes but she blinked them away. She had managed as a single parent when Poppy was born and she would manage just fine having this baby without Rafael's involvement, she told herself firmly. Being financially secure would help.

She'd considered refusing the money he'd agreed to pay her, but although it might restore her pride, which had taken such a battering, she could not let her children grow up in poverty. Rafael had made it clear he did not want his baby, but he was prepared to provide financial support.

His rejection of his child had forced her to accept that the closeness she'd sensed between them had been an illusion. By rejecting their baby he had also rejected her, and it hurt even though she knew she should have expected it. At the start he had warned her not to fall in love with him, and it was her own fault that she'd given him her heart only for him to trample all over it.

Refusing to wallow in any more self-pity,

she went to find Poppy in the nursery. Sofia was there, with Ana and Inez, and she looked shocked when she saw Juliet.

'Has something happened? You look terrible.'

So Rafael hadn't told his sister.

Juliet forced a bright smile. 'I must be coming down with a cold—or maybe hay fever has made my eyes red.'

Sofia looked unconvinced, especially when Juliet went on to explain that she was taking her daughter back to England.

'Poppy is due to start nursery in a month, and I think it will be better for her to begin her schooling in England.'

'Is Rafael going with you?'

'You'll have to ask him.' Juliet avoided her sister-in-law's gaze and started taking Poppy's clothes out of the drawers, ready to be packed.

'I don't know what's happened between you and my brother,' Sofia muttered while the children played. 'But I do know that Rafael has never been as happy as he has for the past months. He needs you, Juliet.'

Juliet bit her lip, fighting back tears. 'He doesn't need anyone. Rafael is...'

'A flesh and blood man—even though he lets people think he has ice in his veins. I *know* him,' Sofia said intensely. 'He bleeds when he is wounded, the same as the rest of us.' She grimaced at Juliet. 'I thought you were different from the other women. I thought you would fight for him—but you're giving up on him.'

Now was not the time to tell Sofia about the baby, Juliet thought wearily as she stood in her dressing room and picked out a few clothes to take with her. Her flight to London was later that afternoon and Rafael had said in his text that he would have the bulk of her belongings sent to Ferndown House.

Not that she would be needing ball gowns or the sexy negligees that she'd bought to replace her horrible old pyjamas. She would only need maternity clothes in the months ahead.

Her hand strayed to her flat stomach. It was hard to believe that a new life was developing inside her. Despite everything, her heart clenched with love for this baby. Another little one who would need her to fulfil the roles of both parents.

The positive pregnancy test had made her sink to her knees on the bathroom floor, her shock mixed with trepidation about Rafael's reaction to the news. She'd guessed he might be angry for a while, but he had been so much worse, so grimly adamant that he didn't want this baby.

She frowned, thinking of that strange comment he'd made. *'What if I am my father's son?'* She did not understand what he'd meant, and she was too tired and defeated to try and work it out.

She looked at the clock and realised that Hector would be waiting for her in his study. She read to him every day, and they were on the final chapter of the latest book they had enjoyed. It would be the last time she would read to him and her eyes brimmed again.

Never would she have believed when Rafael had brought her to the Casillas mansion that she would become fond of the elderly man.

Hector was in his study, but he shook his head when she picked up the book from his desk. 'Rafael came to see me last evening.' His shoulders sagged and he suddenly looked old and frail. 'I was shocked by what he told me.'

Juliet waited for Hector to mention her pregnancy, but what he said next sent a judder of shock through her.

'He explained why he married you. That it was a fake marriage to meet my stipulation that he must be married before I would make him CEO. I suspected as much,' Hector said heavily. 'But I could not really believe that Rafael's ambition would drive him to such an action.'

'We did a terrible thing,' Juliet whispered, shame rolling through her. 'I agreed to the marriage deal because I needed the money. It wasn't only Rafael. I am as much to blame for pretending that our marriage was real.'

His grandfather looked at her closely. 'You defend him?'

'I am his wife. It is my duty to defend my husband.'

Hector nodded. 'And for you the marriage wasn't fake, was it?'

'No.' To her horror Juliet heard her voice crack and she couldn't hold back her tears. 'Thank you,' she choked when Hector handed her a box of tissues.

'I do not think it was fake marriage for my grandson either. Last night Rafael looked more

troubled than I have ever known him to be.'
Hector sighed. 'I was wrong to insist that he
choose a bride. I do believe that Rafael is the
right person to succeed me, but any position
of power can be a lonely place. I was lucky
enough to have the support of my dear wife,
until her death three years ago. Rafael had no
one. I hoped that by forcing him to marry I
could make him realise that there is more to
life than his ruthless ambition.'

Hector patted Juliet's hand.

'Clearly something has happened to cause
a rift between you. Is there no way to resolve
the issue?'

She shook her head, remembering Rafael's
look of abject horror when she'd told him she
was pregnant. 'He doesn't want me and he certainly doesn't love me.'

'How can you be so sure?'

'He's never said so.'

But she thought of the vase of roses he had
placed by her bed yesterday morning. He must
have picked them from the garden before he'd
gone to work, while she had been asleep. And
last week he had spent two hours helping her
search for the gold locket containing photos

of her parents that she'd lost. When he had eventually found it on the pool terrace he had painstakingly fixed the broken clasp on the chain. But did those kind gestures and dozens more like them mean that he cared about her?

'Have you told Rafael how you feel about him?' Hector asked gently.

Even if she did find the courage to admit her love to Rafael he wouldn't want her now that she was pregnant, Juliet thought as she left Hector's study. Perhaps he was so against having a child because he thought he would feel trapped. He had looked so furious, but as she thought back to when she had announced her pregnancy she remembered there had been another emotion in his eyes. There had been fear.

*'What if I am my father's son?'*

She frowned. His father had been a violent bully who had beaten Rafael when he was a little boy. Surely he couldn't think…?

Rafael ran his hand over the thick stubble on his jaw. He guessed he should shave, maybe change out of the clothes that he'd worn for the past twenty-four hours. He tipped the last of the cognac out of the bottle into his glass and contemplated the effort of getting out of his chair, where he had been sprawled ever since he had walked into the penthouse, and decided that the only way to escape his personal hell was to drink himself into oblivion.

Hell had got even blacker when he'd looked at his watch a couple of hours ago and realised that Juliet would be on the Casillas jet heading for London. Heading away from him, and a good job too. She and her cute little daughter would be fine living at Ferndown House without him. And as for the baby. *His baby.* It…he—Juliet was sure she was expecting a boy, and maybe she had an instinctive mother's knowledge—would be well provided for.

Rafael had his own money from the property portfolio he'd built up. His fortune didn't match his family's billions, but he didn't much care right now. Besides he wasn't a Casillas. And he sure as hell didn't want to be a Mendoza. The truth was that he was a mess.

He moved his hand up from his jaw to his cheek and swore when his skin felt wet. He'd get over this, he assured himself. He'd get over *her.* Although it would help if he wasn't being haunted by a vision of her standing by the window, silhouetted against the fading light.

The vision came closer to him and wrinkled her pretty nose. 'Are you drunk?'

'If I am, it's no business of yours,' he growled. 'You should be on a plane.'

'About that...'

She knelt in front of his chair and pushed her long hair over her shoulders. Her perfume stole around him and he gripped his glass so tightly in his fingers that he was surprised it didn't shatter.

'I've decided to stay.'

He glared at her, because it was that or kiss her, and kissing her led to all sorts of trouble—like making love in the shower the one and only time he'd forgotten to use protection.

'Stay where?'

'At the Casillas mansion—or here.' She shrugged. 'A tent on the beach? I don't know. It doesn't matter as long as I'm with you.'

Rafael felt his heart kick hard in his chest. *Fear*, he recognised. Fear that he wasn't strong enough to send her away even though he knew he must.

'The only problem with your plan, *chiquita*,'

he drawled, 'is that I don't want you. Surely you've realised that by now?'

'I've realised a great many things,' she told him seriously. 'For one thing I've realised that you are a liar.'

He swore, but it didn't stop her leaning forward until her face was inches from his and putting her hands flat on his chest.

'You are making a fool of yourself,' he said harshly. 'Are you really going to beg on your knees for me to take you back?'

'If I have to. But as I never left you can't really take me back.'

There was a hint of laughter in her voice. *Laughter.* He'd accepted that he would never laugh again, and he would have told her that grim truth if she hadn't pressed her lips to his mouth so that he couldn't speak, couldn't think. He couldn't do anything but keep his mouth tightly closed until she got the message.

But it got harder and harder to resist the sweet seduction of her lips. He dropped the glass and put his hands on her shoulders to push her away. How, then, did she end up sitting on his lap, her hand holding his jaw, his hands tangled in the silken fall of her hair?

Her mouth was his downfall and his delight, and with a savage groan he took charge of the kiss and drank from her as if he had been lost in a desert and she was life-giving water.

'I love you.'

*Dios*. He stared into her eyes and watched a tear slide down her cheek. 'I told you not to. Why didn't you pay attention, you little idiot? I'm no good for you, and I'm certainly no good for that baby of yours.'

He tried to set her away from him but he was trapped by her hair wrapped around his fingers and by something invisible that wrapped itself around his heart.

'The baby is yours too. *Ours.*'

He sat upright and cupped her chin in both his hands so that she couldn't look away from him. 'I've told you what my father was—what he did to me. Suppose I am like him? I have a temper like Ivan did. I've learned to control it, but what if I *lose* control? What if I lash out and hurt the baby? Or you?'

'You won't.'

'I won't take the risk.'

Juliet stood up and walked across the room.

*Finally,* Rafael thought bleakly. *Finally she sees the monster.*

'Do you think I would risk my children's safety and wellbeing?' she said fiercely. 'I have seen you with Poppy and your nieces—your patience and your caring. You are not the evil man your father was.'

'How do you *know*?' he said, struggling to speak past the lump in his throat. 'How can you have such faith in me?'

She smiled and he rocked back on his heels, blinded by her beauty, humbled by her courage.

'Because I *know* you. I know you are capable of love and I understand why you are afraid. You are a good man, Rafael. You don't need to prove yourself to anyone, least of all me. I love you with all my heart. I need you, and so does our baby.'

He stared at her while his thoughts rearranged themselves and hope slipped stealthily into his heart. When he walked towards her he saw a shadow of vulnerability in her eyes that killed him.

'Say something,' she whispered. 'Can you love me just a little?'

'*Querida*—' His voice broke and he reached for her, hauling her into his arms and holding her against his chest where his heart was doing its best to burst through his skin. '*Te amo, mi corazón.*'

He kissed her wet eyelashes, the tip of her nose, her lips that parted beneath his as she kissed him back with all that sweetness and light that was his wife, the love of his life.

'I don't know when it began,' he said, resting his chin on the top of her head. 'You got to me in a way no other woman had ever done. You defended me, and no one had ever done that before.'

'It wasn't love at first sight, then?' she said ruefully.

'I was a blind fool—but you showed me that you are beautiful, inside and out.' He looked into her eyes and read her unspoken question. 'It ripped my heart out when I sent you away but I thought it was for the best.'

His heart gave another kick when she held his hand against her stomach, where the new life they had created together linked them inextricably.

'I will love our baby, and Poppy, but more than anything I will love *you, mi Julieta*, for the rest of our lives. For always and for ever.'

# EPILOGUE

RAFAEL STOOD IN the hallway of Ferndown House and watched a troop of small girls wearing pink leotards run out of the room which Juliet had turned into a dance studio. Their parents were waiting in the lobby and there was general chaos while coats were found and ballet shoes were swapped for trainers.

'Your last class for a while,' he said to his wife when the house was quiet again.

'Yes, it will be nice to have a few weeks off, and the babies should arrive any day now.' She patted her swollen belly. 'In a couple of years' time I'll have two more pupils.'

He shook his head. 'I can't believe there will be another set of twin girls in the family besides Sofia's girls. Can you imagine the mayhem when we all get together at Christmas?'

Rafael looked at his son, who had run in from the garden holding a football. Diego

Casillas was three years old, and chasing him was his big sister Poppy, who had just turned seven.

'Your grandfather will enjoy having the whole family to stay. You know how he dotes on all the children. And your mother will spoil them,' Juliet said serenely.

She was tired now, at the end of her third pregnancy, but Rafael thought she had never looked more beautiful.

They had made the decision to live in England after Diego was born. When Rafael had become CEO of the Casillas Group after Hector had retired he had insisted on sharing the role with his half-brother. Francisco now worked from the company's offices in Valencia, and Rafael was based in London. He and Juliet wanted their own home, where they could bring up their growing family, and Ferndown House was filled with love and laughter.

Especially love, Rafael mused as he drew Juliet into his arms and she lifted her face for his kiss. He adored her, and told her so daily. The bright blue sapphire and diamond ring he had slipped onto her finger next to her wedding band was just one token of his deep and abiding love for this woman who had brought him out of the darkness into her golden light.

'It feels like there's a riot going on in there,' he murmured when a tiny foot kicked his hand where his fingers were splayed possessively on Juliet's bump.

'Yes, I think your new daughters are ready to meet their daddy.' She looped her arms around his neck. 'You know what's supposed to bring on labour…?'

'Señora Casillas—are you suggesting that we…?' He whispered the rest of the sentence in her ear and she giggled.

'Yes, please, Señor Casillas, my love.'

Love and laughter. He couldn't ask for more, Rafael thought.

And three days later, when he held two little bundles whom they'd named Lola and Clara in his arms, he knew he was the luckiest man in the world.

\* \* \* \* \*

# LET'S TALK
## *Romance*

For exclusive extracts, competitions and special offers, find us online:

f facebook.com/millsandboon

⬤ @millsandboonuk

🐦 @millsandboon

Or get in touch on 0844 844 1351*

For all the latest titles coming soon, visit millsandboon.co.uk/nextmonth